Dad is the center around which we all turn. Aren't we almost the all-American family? We eat our meals together whenever we can, balanced, all-American meals: protein, starch, and vegetable. Apple pie and peach cobbler and the like for dessert. . . . My parents come to every single one of my basketball games, and Dad goes crazy with joy whenever I pop one in. At ten o'clock most nights they know where their child is. As a family we've got it made. So what is this all about? How could Dad take off for Alaska without us? . . . We are the two people he loves most.

SHEILA SOLOMON KLASS

PAGE FOUR

BANTAM BOOKS
TORONTO · NEW YORK · LONDON · SYDNEY · AUCKLAND

RL 6, IL age 12 and up

PAGE FOUR

A Bantam Book / published by arrangement with
Charles Scribner's Sons

PRINTING HISTORY

Scribner's edition published November 1986

The song, "(Let Me Be Your) Teddy Bear," by Bernie Lowe and Kal Mann,
is copyright © 1957 by Gladys Music, Inc. Copyright renewed, assigned to
Chappell & Co., Inc. (Intersong Music, Publisher). International copyright
secured. All rights reserved. Used by permission.

"One More Renaissance" and "Cleave Together, Cleave Apart": Lyrics
and music by Judy Klass. Copyright © 1984 by Judy Klass. Used by
permission. All rights reserved.

The Starfire logo is a registered trademark of Bantam Books, Inc.
Registered in U.S. Patent and Trademark Office and elsewhere.

Bantam edition / January 1988

ISBN 0-553-26901-1

Published simultaneously in the United States and Canada

PRINTED IN THE UNITED STATES OF AMERICA

O   C 9 8 7 6 5 4 3 2 1

For my sister, Marilyn Koster, with love
and
In memory of Milton Koster,
who bought me my first
typewriter

PAGE 4

COLLEGE APPLICATION FOR FRESHMAN
ADMISSION

WRITING SAMPLE

ALL THE GRADES, SCORES, AND RECOMMENDATIONS YOU
HAVE SUPPLIED EARLIER TELL US A LIMITED AMOUNT
ABOUT YOU. PLEASE USE THE SPACE ON THIS PAGE
(AND AS MANY OTHER PAGES AS YOU REQUIRE) TO TELL
US THINGS ABOUT YOURSELF THAT ARE NOT EVIDENT
FROM THE REST OF YOUR APPLICATION.

IN THE PAST, APPLICANTS HAVE USED THIS OPPORTU-
NITY IN MANY DIFFERENT WAYS. SOME HAVE WRITTEN
ABOUT SCHOOL, FAMILY EVENTS, COMMUNITY OR WORLD
SITUATIONS THAT HAVE AFFECTED THEM DEEPLY, INTEL-
LECTUAL EXPERIENCES, MEANINGFUL INTERESTS, PER-
SONAL GOALS, OR TOPICS THAT ARE WHOLLY PRODUCTS
OF THE IMAGINATION. THERE IS NO ONE FORMAT, NO
SINGLE WAY TO HANDLE THIS ASSIGNMENT. WRITE
ABOUT WHAT IS IMPORTANT TO YOU AND YOU WILL
TELL US MUCH ABOUT YOURSELF.

I t is a winter afternoon and the ground is hard-packed with snow, the sky stone-colored. I am running backward through the high school's main hall horsing around with my friend Bean (a.k.a. Robert Rogers, but called Bean because he sprouts so fast). I've got hold of his gross new zebra-striped knapsack, which he insists is some magical new waterproof material. "I'm going to bury it in the snow as a scientific test," I tease him.

"Come on, Dave. All my books are in there. And the two *Star Trek* novels you lent me."

"Why are you worried, if it really is waterproof?"

"Experiments with snow can be very dangerous." He's mysterious, as if he really knows something.

I figure it's a stall so he can grab the knapsack. "Dangerous how?" My eyes never leave him. He's built for basketball, a Lipizzaner, graceful at prancing and high-jumping but with orangutan hands.

He lunges and misses. Crafty though he is, I outmaneuver him with my nifty footwork. "Sir Francis Bacon in the seventeenth century—"

I groan but that doesn't stop Bean.

"—died of a chill he caught while stuffing a chicken with snow to see if that would stop decay."

"You made that up." I juke to the left.

"I swear. Ask anyone. Bacon is the guy who

3

argued that scientists should investigate observable facts, not theories. Induction, it's called, and it got him into trouble in his day."

"Fascinating." I shift the knapsack behind me.

"Unfortunately, this try at refrigeration was his first experiment. Short career," Bean says.

"I guess that night the undertaker brought home the Bacon," I say, and he clutches his gut and gargles. I nod, accepting this tribute modestly. Surely, since the seventeenth century, someone else must have made that joke.

I know he's not making all this up. He has that kind of mind. He collects natural and scientific and math data the way a bee collects pollen; it all sticks to him. He has a head jammed with facts, but he can't put them down easily on paper. My mind sponges up the soft knowledge: languages, lit, arts, and anything about sports. I do my thinking best on paper, and it pleases me to be able to do it with style. I get the same rush out of putting ideas down perfectly in writing that I get running down the hardwood and pouring in a key basket. Anyway, both Bean and I read all sorts of kooky material, from sci fi, *The National Enquirer,* and comic books to the good stuff. Long ago we made a pact that we'd show the world that jocks can be smart! That's how come we're friends; we *think* even though we play basketball. Together we make one great student.

"I didn't know that's how Bacon bought it," I admit. "He's the one some people believe really wrote Shakespeare's plays."

"I knew *some* big ham did it," Bean says, and I take the opportunity while he's yukking at his own joke to slip out the front door. While I'm moving down the steps, I catch sight of my mother sitting in her BMW—motor running.

4

My mother, Ann Smith, should be called Mrs. Ecology. She collects newspapers and bottles and cans for recycling. She conserves water. She turns lights off. Usually the motor does not idle in the car of the woman who chews out the school bus driver if he waits for me with his engine running. (Even though she's right, it's embarrassing.) In fact, she's never done this pollution bit before that I can remember. I release the miracle-fiber zebra to Bean and call to her, "What's up?" Edison Regional High School has buses going back and forth at practically all hours. In good weather we bike home, or walk. Sometimes eight or nine of us cram into someone's car. I hate being picked up. I'm an only child and my father has warned me (privately) about being babied.

Mom and I have this old routine we fool around with: about a very rich lady who arrives at a swank hotel in her Rolls and tells the doorman to carry up first her suitcases, then her jewels, then her furs, then her son. "I'm so sorry, Madam," says the doorman. "Can't your son walk?" "Of course he can," she snaps. "Thank goodness he doesn't have to!"

"I'm so sorry, Madam," I put it to Mom. "Can't your son walk?"

I wait for the punch line. Nothing comes; she just sits there.

"I would've brought your little David home, Mrs. Smith," Bean says. "I wouldn't leave him to catch it in the snow like Francis Bacon did."

Bean expects her to say "Who?" so he can tell her the whole frozen chicken story, but she seems not to hear him. She sits up rigid, the motor going. I notice some peculiar things. She has a kerchief on her head and she's not wearing make-up. She looks beat.

"Get in, Dave," she says. "Let's go get a hot drink."

I toss my gear in back. "Can we at least give Bean a drop home?"

"Not today. The school bus will be along in a few minutes. Sorry. Please, Dave. Get in."

"See you." Bean's right eyebrow moves up slightly to signal it's okay. He knows something is up.

"Sorry," Mom says to him again, and then she takes off along the icy driveway, wheels squealing like we are in the Indy Five Hundred. We head way off, not to the local diner but to one of those stucco palazzos that are stuck-o all over the New Jersey main roads. New Jersey is the pits. Mugged New Yorkers come here to live. Fear sells the real estate. And every workday all the commuters leave their vulnerables behind the Palisades and take off for the dangerous city.

I sit there beside her suffering from lockjaw. I don't say a single word because I know I do not want to hear what is coming. I know that, I just know it. The vibes are bad. I see her hands tight with tension pressing the wheel. It's not necessary. The BMW drives like a baby carriage. She is sending out distress signals and I am picking them up like a radar screen.

Mom is an interesting lady, a Quaker from an old Philadelphia family of Quakers (her brother, my uncle Kurt, was a conscientious objector during the Vietnam War). Quakerism, Mom says, is more than a religion; it's a whole way of living, a style, and a mental attitude. She does not go to church. She believes in the "Inward Light," which means divine

6

guidance from the Holy Spirit straight to her heart. She is also opposed to taking oaths, and to war. Dad is Presbyterian and he does go to church occasionally. Neither one tries to change the other, and I have been left to choose my own way. I like the Quaker ideas, but they are a bit weird. I'd be embarrassed to talk about them to other kids. Bean knows and he finds it interesting, but that's just Bean.

Oddly, this Quaker lady was prom queen of her Main Line high school, which really makes me laugh—it's so out of character, except that she's gorgeous in the prom pictures—and then she came to New York and Barnard College where she majored in science. Botany was her special interest, and she is the world's greatest gardener even today. If she watered a seed in the Kalahari Desert it would start a Green Revolution. She crossed Broadway and ran into Dad (literally; it was dark) on the steps of Low Library and that was that. He was a graduate student; he only needed one glimpse of her by starlight, he says, to claim her for his own. It's a romantic story, and when I was a kid I used to want to hear it over and over. She never really got a chance to work because right out of college she had me. "I do the supporting around here," Dad likes to say. He's from Oak Park, Illinois, the birthplace of Ernest Hemingway, who is the Papa of American macho. That's a running joke in our house; whenever Dad thinks something he's been asked to do is unmanly he simply reminds us where he's from. Oak Park men don't carry out the garbage. "Must be something in the water there," Mom teases him. She really didn't mind not having a career. I was so *fascinating,* she says, she was glad to stay home and raise me. Fascinating is a little heavy, but after all, she is my mom.

7

She loves kids. After me she wanted more, but Dad insisted that I was enough. A terrific son! (I couldn't have agreed with him more.) The world is overpopulated, Dad argued. Okay, let's adopt, Mom said. Well—he came up with other reservations: their constant moving around, the cost of college educations, the uncertainty factor in adoption; a dozen other reasons. Mom got the message. I was it! She was sorry, but he felt so strongly about it she let it ride.

That's why she loves working in our town library. She's a volunteer assisting Miss McKuen, the head librarian, who is a character right out of Dickens. Mom works in the children's room.

Mom can do millions of things; she is probably the most all-around competent person I know. She cooks, sews, does carpentry, gardens, and can turn any dump into a home in a short time. Civil engineers end up in oddball places. "She builds a nest," Dad says, and it's so. Whenever he has to move on a job she makes it practically painless. Home is where she is.

She's really smart. For years she beat me in chess though I worked on my game a lot. Now I'm a match for her, but she still destroys me once in a while with an unexpected sneaky powerhouse gambit. So probably she could have had a career, been a great somebody. She is. A great mother.

Driving is something else she is good at, and I'm really grateful for that this dangerous winter day. Despite the ice on the New Jersey roads, we make it. Black coffee for Mom; hot chocolate, my favorite drink, for me.

That was my last cup of hot chocolate. I'll never touch the stuff again. Before that cupful I was living in paradise and I didn't know it. Maybe

8

that's true for everyone; maybe paradise always just *was* and you only know afterward when you've lost it. What a creepy idea for the Now Generation. Now was then. It's gone.

She just sits at the table, her head drooping on her neck like a pinched flower, her soft blond hair messy under her kerchief, her lips pale. My mom is a small woman—petite, she says—fair, fresh-faced, with clear gray eyes and a creamy skin. Her genes save me from acne. A Sandra Dee type. Her style is *well-groomed* from early morning on. When every normal person like me is in bed yawning and turning over, she's already showering *et cetera*. We've been known to have differences over this. I favor late rising and minimal washing but maximum Old Spice under the arms. Casual is in, I give her the word. Queen Isabella of Spain had only three baths in her life: at birth, marriage, and death, and it didn't do her a bit of harm. (I wonder if Columbus sat downwind of her. Nobody says.)

But at this moment Mom is almost unrecognizable. I guess misery provides its own disguises.

"Your father is going away," she manages to say finally, halfway through her coffee.

That's a shocker, all right.

"Where?" My father's career often calls for him taking off for a few months on various projects. From elementary school on up we just shut up the house and went along. Last year we were in D.C. for four months. My grades are good and I'm young for my class, so shuttling around didn't do any damage except, of course, I only got to play half a season of team basketball for Edison during my sophomore year. The one coming up is going to be the big one. My plan is to earn my major letter.

We have a family agreement now that I should have several years of stability in school, a launching pad to blast me up into a super college. After all, they met on Morningside Heights and had great years, and the same, we hope, is in the cards for me. Some families believe in owning the best cars and that's what they focus on and mostly talk about. Some families talk about church and religion. Our family believes in going for the best education whatever it costs. Knowledge and contact with good minds is the point; that, to my parents and therefore to me, means a top college. Maybe we're snobs, but it's better to be college snobs than car snobs. So, the game plan is to stay right here in Cloverdale till Edison Regional High School gives me the old heave. Right into the Ivy, the best!

Mom wets her lips with her tongue. "He's going to Alaska. To live for good." She is sitting right across from me, two feet away, with a red Formica table between us, but that table could be the Great Wall of China, she's so distant.

"He can't do that. I'm going to finish high school here."

"You don't understand," she says. "He's not taking you. Or me."

I consider this incredible statement for a second, and, stupidly, I take a mouthful of hot chocolate, which tastes like sweetened mud. Then I gallop to the men's room where I barf till my ribs beg me to stop. I wash my face at the dribbly faucet and mop up with a paper towel. This palazzo has peasant facilities. The towel sandpapers my face. Amazingly weak, I make my way back to the table.

"You all right?" Mom asks anxiously. "You're terribly pale."

"Ptomaine." I push the Nestlé cup and saucer away, and then I sit and study her from under my lids and sideways trying to figure out what's driven her bonkers. It must be middle age. She's thirty-eight. Last month I read some magazine article in the doctor's office about women getting strange when they get older. It has to do with hormones and stuff. Some women grow mustaches. I search her face for hair. Nothing. I sit there wishing I knew more about biology, but I don't get to take the advanced course till I'm a senior.

So there she is sitting and fantasizing about my father, David Smith, Sr. (for whom I'm named, surprise, surprise), a great guy, a normal husband and father. He's handsome, he's shrewd, and he earns a good living. He was a three-letter man at college and he was also Phi Beta Kappa, which means smart. A tall man, six feet two inches, his college nickname was "Big Man." I'm incredibly proud of him. I intend—and he intends for me—to grow up much like him.

What's pushed her off her track? Dad is the center around which we all turn. Aren't we almost the all-American family? We eat our meals together whenever we can, balanced, all-American meals: protein, starch, and vegetable. Apple pie and peach cobbler and the like for dessert. The way they eat in Oak Park, Illinois. None of that sauerbraten or pumpernickel Mom's family ate. Dad claims he was sick for weeks after their engagement dinner. "I'm a white-bread man," he says. Grandma Smith taught Mom all his favorite dishes and they are good. We stay away from peculiar stuff. We're American; we eat American; we travel American. That's my Dad's style.

We hike together and hunt mushrooms. My

11

parents come to every single one of my basketball games and Dad goes crazy with joy whenever I pop one in. At ten o'clock most nights they know where their child is. As a family we've got it made. So what is this all about? How could Dad take off for Alaska without us, her and me both? We are the two people he loves most.

"I don't believe you," I say. "I just don't believe you. He wouldn't do that. Not Dad."

She begins to laugh this weird, low laugh in her chest, ratatatat, like a machine gun.

"Mom," I say uneasily. "Mom?" I am so glad we are in the palazzo and not in our local diner. The characters here don't know us.

She stops.

"Why would he want to go and live in Alaska without us? That's crazy."

I get no moment of grace, no time to brace my body for the knockout punch.

"He's fallen in love with someone," she says softly. She is shredding her napkin like it's classified information. "He wants to make a new life with her."

"Why didn't he tell me himself?"

"He wanted to. I thought it might be easier on you if I broke it to you first. He's at home now packing and waiting for you."

I look at her closely. "Did you know about this—before?"

She looks at her shreds. "No," she says, her voice a whisper. "I refused to know about it."

"I want to go home."

"Dave—" She touches my wrist very lightly. "Wait a while. Sit here quietly and collect yourself. Don't go running in on him defenseless. It will hurt you too much."

"I want to go home and hear it from the Big Man himself."

We break the speed laws going home. Mom has never been this way. I say nothing. I pray and we make it. He is upstairs in their bedroom still packing, moving around a lot. He has a heavy tread.

"Go hear it from the Big Man," Mom says. She makes no move to come along. I start to climb that long, polished-wood staircase alone. "Be brave," she says softly behind me.

I do not know how.

There he is, the Big Man, and by the looks of things he's almost finished packing. He's really built: one-eighty pounds on a lean frame. Dad and I look amazingly alike, like twins, one of whom was caught in a time warp: tall, tight-muscled, brown curly hair cut short, brown eyes, straight noses; maybe not spectacular but definitely noticeable. I love to look in the mirror and see how much I resemble him. Just now I'm in a growth spurt. I'm exactly six feet tall and I can't wait until I pass the Big Man on the way up. "Hello, Tiny," I'll say, after the measuring ceremony, which we do in the living room against the door frame. "Hello, Petite." It will drive him wild.

It's something special to have a father who's a winner, who goes for what he wants and usually gets it. His own father died when he was eight— drowned while fishing in Lake Michigan—but he left enough money so Grandma could live comfortably and devote herself to her son and daughter. Grandma adored Dad. (Poor Aunt Rosalie couldn't compete with that old charisma; she moved off to be on her own as soon as she could; I hardly know her.) Grandma saw Dad through his college years and his marriage to Mom, and then when he was safe, she died peacefully in her sleep. Money was left for him and for Rosalie, and there's even some

14

extra in trust for posterity, which turns out to be yours truly. The Big Man is on a constant roll.

"Hello, David."

"Dad."

"Mother spoken to you?"

I nod.

"Sit down." He points to the bed. It's a no-no but he's got the armchair all piled up with luggage, so I sit on the flag, on the bicentennial patchwork quilt that is Mom's pride. It took her two years to sew, every stitch handsewn.

He's got a thick, twisted gold bracelet on display on his wrist. It's new and shiny and way out of character for Oak Park, Illinois. I stare at it and he notices. His face reddens.

Peculiar. I feel as if I am outside myself watching him and me from a great distance, a kind of human zoom lens recording the scene forever: *David Smith, Jr., his farewell to his father.* A historic scene.

There's a pause as he searches for a favorable stance before the opening tap off. "What can I say?" he begins.

A fumble.

"I'm not writing your dialogue." I refuse to retrieve. I wait, but he doesn't take another shot at it. "I want to hear it from you."

Now he does look me in the eye. "I'm going away, moving to Alaska. You and your mother are remaining here."

"You mean you're leaving us—here?"

"You might say that."

"Why didn't *you* say it?" It's spooky, but that moment is the first time in my life that I really understood that one day I will die. Me, Dave Smith, a solid, terrific guy, so healthy I can do fifty push-ups without noticing. A chill ripples along my spinal cord, and I shiver. "Stuff it," I say, and put my head in my hands.

"I hate hurting you and your mother. I'd do anything in the world I could to make it easier."

I give him the eye. Anything in the world— except stay. I don't have to say it. He begins to lay ties into the big crammed leather bag. It's something to do. The silence creates a vacuum, and after a while he jumps in. "There won't be any money problems," he says. "I've made all the arrangements." The last tie has been laid away.

"We aren't dead yet," I tell him, looking up.

"What?"

"You sound like the ad for Riverside Memorial Chapel." I deepened my voice. "*We make all the arrangements.* Only you can't *make all the arrangements* for living people."

"I mean that I've taken care of both of you financially."

"We don't want your money."

"Yes, you do. You need it."

I hate that because it's true. "Anyway, it will make you feel better if you pay."

"Perhaps. But you will need it."

"Stuff it."

He stands still for a moment, his big hands open in front of him as if he's signing: *How can I help it?*

We face each other in that silence, the man I love most in the world and I, his namesake.

"Why?" I ask.

He inhales a tankful. "I want to start a new life. With someone *else.*" He is embarrassed; his eyes shift away, but there's no escape.

16

"That's what Mom said. I still need to know why."

"I'm in love. When someone falls in love—"

"Stuff it."

A nervous hand runs through the short curly hair. "Can't you say anything else? You're a junior in high school and you've only got one expression?" He's edgy, the way guilty people are. I happen to recognize the feeling myself. "Try speaking English," he advises me.

"Slang is English. Substandard, but English."

He tolerates that with a super sigh, one of those Shakespearian air blasts as if *he* has troubles. Good thing I don't breathe my feelings at this moment; my sigh would untilt the axis and tremble the earth.

It sinks in on him that I am not letting him off. No help is coming from me. He lights up a cigarette and begins. "I know you don't understand this now, Dave. Someday you might. It's not that I don't care for you and your mother. I do, and I always will. But I love Laurie—differently. I don't know how to explain it to you. I have to have my chance with her."

"Too bad you're not a Moslem," I say. "You could have four wives." I am absolutely freaked by this explanation. It's so cornball. And Laurie? *Laurie? I know her!* She is the programmer in his office, a cute redhead with a big smile and big boobs. She knows everything there is to know about computers. She's a big Springsteen fan. "Laurie!" I say in shock. "Laurie? You're too old for her. She listens to Springsteen."

"So do I on occasion," he says, and he really squirms.

I am totally amazed. In the attic is an old guitar

17

he used to fool with in college. He played Dylan and Pete Seeger and the Beatles' early stuff. He stopped playing the guitar once we bought this house and moved into it. In fact, he stored it away in the attic. He always puts down everything new in music as junk. Nothing can compare with the old folkies.

"I don't understand how you can do this, Dad."

He rubs his hands over his face. "It's not easy." Bringing a pile of socks to the suitcase, he bends over and begins stuffing them in corners. They are all socks I know: white, thick sweat socks with blue bands, gray wool hiking socks, thin black, navy, and tan everyday socks. These socks are part of my life, too. Everything going into that suitcase is. I want to say: *Unpack what you are taking. You are stealing from our family.*

"Of all the people in my life I respected you pretty much the most. I just don't understand how you can do this. Remember how you told me that because Grandpa drowned you grew up feeling somehow that he had run out on you? Why did he have to go fishing and die? And when you were a kid you used to think he did it on purpose?"

"Yes," my father says. "That's so."

"And *he* couldn't help himself. He drowned!"

"I can't help myself either, David. I have to go."

"Then you know how I feel. You're running out on us. On me."

"You're not eight years old. You're twice the age I was when it happened. You're almost out of high school. Before you know it you'll be going to college. You're almost a man. I hoped you would be able to understand better than I did."

18

"I'll never understand running out on someone."

"I would take you with me—with us—David, but your mother needs you."

"With you? So Laurie can be my stepmother? What a joke! 'Born to Run' is the right song for you two."

"Dave—" He reaches the hand with the bracelet toward me. Yuck.

"Keep off." I almost punch him. "No trespassing. Private property." I stand there thinking about it. "It's not as if you and Mom were fighting a lot or anything," I say desperately.

"It's not your mother's fault. It's nobody's fault. It just happened."

"Boy," I say to him, "that's a hot excuse. Catch me covering with that when I'm in trouble. Why did you fail chemistry? It just happened. How did you smash your stereo? It just happened."

It doesn't get a rise out of him.

"These things repeat themselves in families," I mumble, remembering a pop psychology article I just read. "Desertion, alcoholism, child abuse, suicide."

"David?"

"I'm cool," I say. "I'm not going to do something desperate." I have to draw a little blood. I can't just let him go. "You're not worth it," I say.

"Watch your mouth," he warns.

I'm beyond his warnings. "Have you ever felt that your life is a replay?" I ask him. "I mean, Mom was the prettiest young girl around when you met her. You used to say so yourself all the time when I was a kid. You just get to do it over and over?" To my horror my voice is going up, getting shrill, the kid in me crying out at him.

19

"That's mean, son, and unworthy of you."

"Mean but true." That *son* is a knife to the major blood supplier in my chest. I feel weak. I have to get out of there quick. "You've got no right to talk to me about unworthy." I start to leave.

"Want to say good-bye?" he asks my back.

"Nope. I don't wish you *good anything.*" I walk out of there real stiff and dignified, almost slow motion, and then quicken my steps to the bathroom where I gag and cough, my face in a towel to muffle sounds. Me, ironstomach Smith, who can keep down the school cafeteria's bread pudding while kids tell me where the leftover bread that's in it came from: trash bins, contagious wards, leprosariums—that last one from Bean. My father delivers one fast one to my gut and it folds. Once I am safe in my bedroom and the door is locked I fall on my bed and bury my head in my quilt, my eyes burning. Eddie Van Halen is doing a solo in my head. The pounding echoes. We aren't criers in our family, none of us, not even Mom. I was brought up to contain my feelings and not make a big fuss. So I lie there, dryness searing my eye sockets.

For a long time thoughts bubble up and then knock each other under like swimmers in a crowded pool. But then one idea surfaces, bobs up, and stays on top.

Teenage suicide is in; the guidance counselor gave a major lecture on the subject two weeks ago. Once guidance gets some topic they chew it to death. Bad metaphor.

Sure, I could just take myself a little walk into that bathroom and slip out one of those Gillette blades he bought me because my face is getting gross and hairy, and I could slit the old wrists. Just one or two deft strokes and then I'm out of it for good.

I see him breaking down the door and finding me there on the fioor. Aaiee! And as my pumper fails I whisper, "You did this. You!" How he suffers! Hot spikes under his toenails couldn't hurt more.

I see Mom and she really suffers. Most of all. And she is innocent.

I can't do that to her. She believes in living, in usefulness and responsibility.

I don't really want to be out of it.

And, besides, I'm scared.

After he loads up the car and drives off into the sunset, I run over to Bean's house. "David?" Mrs. Rogers is surprised to see me. "Robert didn't tell me you were coming over, but I'm glad to see you anyway." She wipes her hands on a checked dish towel and comes to help me with my snow-covered stuff. "Take your boots off," she says, "and walk around in your socks." Mrs. Rogers, except for her bizarre taste in bookbags, is an all-right lady. She's tall and a bit heavy, and her nose turns up at the tip. So does Bean's and his twin sister Riley's.

"He didn't know I was coming, Mrs. Rogers. *I* didn't even know I was coming."

"Let me fix some hot chocolate to warm you," she offers.

"No hot chocolate!" I practically scream it.

"David?"

"Sorry. No thank you, Mrs. Rogers, I do not want a hot chocolate. At this particular time it would probably kill me. I'm allergic. It swells my sinuses and gives me bumps on the bottoms of my feet. Worse than a penicillin reaction."

"I never heard," she starts, but something in my face makes her duck her head and accept my strange story. Dealing with Bean and Riley has taught her a lot.

I go up the worn carpeted stairs. Bean's father is a bookkeeper and his mother clerks in our local bank. They don't have a lot of money. As I'm stepping on their frayed tan carpet it occurs to me how lucky they are. Mr. Rogers could never leave Mrs. Rogers the way Dad left Mom. He wouldn't have the money to do it. His old Chrysler would probably only get as far as Trenton. No one ever runs away to start a new life in Trenton.

These ideas about Bean's parents are all totally ridiculous. This is a really close, religious family. My mind is running amuck.

I latch on to the no-money idea. Perhaps Dad will lose his job and run through all his money, I think. Then he'll have to come back home. We'd take him back, penniless. I'd get a part-time job to help out. Roy Rogers or Burger King. Dunkin' Donuts. No problem.

Riley passes me on the landing. "Hi, David."

"Hi," I say, and I watch her run down the stairs. She is like Bean in many ways: tall, black hair, blue eyes, turned-up nose. She is the cleanest-looking girl I ever saw, something fresh and just-washed about her, especially her hair: long, straight, shiny black hair bouncing on her back as she runs.

I like Riley but I'm not exactly comfortable with girls.

I knock.

"I said later. L-A-T-E-R," Bean spells it out at the top of his voice.

I open the door and a pillow gets me in the gut. "What are you, funny?" I throw it right back at him and go in. His room always looks like laundry day at summer camp: clothes everywhere in piles more or less according to kind. Bean has this theory that closets and drawers delay a person: if all the clothes are out in the open in piles, dressing is fast, like an assembly line. The problem is worn clothes dropped when taken off sometimes get mixed in with the clean ones. But the idea basically appeals to me. I try to talk Mom into it, but she isn't having any. Dressing time is private quiet time, she says, and it's precious. Time to get in touch with yourself, to take stock.

Bean is surprised that it's me. "I thought you were my mother. She wants me to shovel snow and I told her I would, later. When you knocked I was teaching her a lesson: patience. The snow is not going anywhere. What's the hurry?"

"Bean, something's happened."

"I could tell by your mother."

"Yeah. You have to promise to keep it quiet."

"I'm a giraffe. Voiceless. The silent animal. I won't say a word." He collects all these peculiar facts about nature; he's a regular five-and-dime store of information.

"This is serious."

He turns his baby blues on me. "I promise."

"Okay. I—my father—we—" I start, and I can't get it out.

"You did some idiot thing and he grounded you?" Bean guesses. I shake my head. "You did some serious thing and he's going to punish you?" Again I deny it silently. "The cops are after you?" Once more I indicate no.

Bean is on full alert. "Tell."

"My father did something awful," I say, "and no one will punish him."

Bean's face, bulgy-eyed, moves forward on his long neck. "What'd he do, take a bribe? Sand in the concrete? Asbestos in the insulation?"

"Worse."

24

"He poisoned somebody with one of those crazy mushrooms he collects?"

"Worse."

Bean is baffled. "What could be worse? Ah! He buried a body in a foundation—or in a cornerstone, the way gangsters do."

"No. He just took off for Alaska."

"Alaska?"

"Yeah. Without me or Mom. He's got a new girl friend."

"Alaska." Bean can't believe it at first. He collapses on the mountain of tee shirts nearest him. "*Your* father? But your mother is beautiful. He must be nuts."

I nod.

"Sit." He points to jeans and even reaches over to flatten the pile. "Why Alaska?"

"Don't ask me. Maybe because it's far away. He wants to start a new life."

It takes Bean a while to absorb all that. Then he puckers up his mouth like our general science teacher (freshman year), Mrs. Zygoda—we think her lipstick is made of alum—and he begins to speak in her mannered no-nonsense way. "Parents should not be left on their own. They require constant supervision because they are immature. On the evolutionary scale the parent is closest to the original primate. . . ." He stops when he sees it is not doing any good. There are no life signs in me. I have been thoroughly zapped.

"Dave," he says quietly, "I am your friend forever, no matter what. You can count on me." He offers his hand and I slap it gladly.

"What am I going to do?" I ask him. "I can't live without a father. I love—loved—my father. I come home every night and I tell him and her

25

about the day, all the nutty things and stuff. I look forward to that at dinnertime. It's the best time of all. I can't believe he'd do this."

Bean is silent. "Listen," he says finally, and he talks slow because he's working it out, "I can lend you my father whenever you need advice or someone to talk to. He listens okay. Sometimes he falls asleep but if you stop talking he wakes right up and tells you to go on. I know it's not as good as your own father, but it's something. And he does love basketball though he's always been a watcher, not a player like your dad."

"Thanks," I say, "but it's not advice or anything I need. It's just him being there. And he's not going to be there anymore."

"It stinks," Bean says, "but maybe you get used to it."

"I'm going to try." I make up my mind. "I'm going to try to wipe him out of my life like chalk on a blackboard. Not a trace will remain."

Bean looks so sorry I can't stand it. "Speaking of stinks," I say, rising from the piled Levis, "you ought to supply a gas mask when someone sits in here. This is fragrant laundry." I get the same pillow in my gut again.

"This is my room," he says. "I run it my way. I'm building up tolerance for odors."

I'm hurting but I exit laughing.

My mother is waiting for me when I come in from Bean's house. She has just showered and is wearing a rose flannel bathrobe. All my life she has worn robes that color; Dad loved her in them and kept supplying new ones. I remember when I was a little kid up at night, scared or sick, that bright softness meant warmth and safety. Now her pale hair is soft and damp and her face is shiny clean. But suddenly old, bleak. For the first time my mother has the face of a loser. I can't bear to see it.

She is sitting on the couch, her bare feet tucked up under her.

She is smoking a cigarette.

I know we are in serious trouble. My father is the smoker in our house. Long ago, during her college days when she wanted to be grown-up, she smoked too, but when she was pregnant with me she gave it up. It was a struggle. She had withdrawal symptoms: dry mouth, headaches, cramps. She ate a lot and she chewed whole packs of gum, but she'd made up her mind. It was hard with Dad smoking right there alongside her, but she did it. How do I know all this? Propaganda to keep me clean. She wouldn't endanger the baby: me. Now, sixteen years afterward, she sits there puffing away

27

and there is a carton of his Marlboros on the coffee table.

"Dave," she calls to me, "we should talk."

I shed my ski jacket in the entryway along with my boots, and I come in and sit on the rug across from her, avoiding the leather armchair. "The Surgeon General Has Determined that Cigarette Smoking Is Dangerous to Your Health," I say.

"The surgeon general is right. But I can't help myself. It's either slit my wrists, or run out madly screaming at the moon, or smoke."

I am startled. Did I think I was the only one who knew about razor blades and despair? "So run out and scream. It will do us both good."

"Ah, son." She smiles bitterly. "If only I could."

"Okay, Mom. Dish it to me."

"You know I love you—and your father loves you."

"Yeah."

"And what has happened is hard for all of us."

"Oh sure, especially for him. I'm crying for him."

Her eyes stop me. "Hard for him, too," she says, "because if he could do this casually he wouldn't be the person we loved." She raises her hand to stop me. "Just hear me out, just this once, and we won't talk about it again. This is not easy for me either."

I nod.

"Both of us love you. Your father is gone, and what happened is his fault but not altogether. For a long time things have not been good—" She stops till she can get control of her trembling lower lip. "Private things between husband and wife were bad between us. We were not close anymore. But I wouldn't acknowledge it." She grinds out the butt and takes time to tap out a new one and light it. I focus on the nap of the rug, hand-brushing it in one direction. I've got a lot of it done before she picks up again. "I was brought up to put a good face on things and hope for the best. To be optimistic. Maybe I confused faith with wishful thinking, I don't know. I guess I was just waiting it out, hoping."

This whole spiel is making me feel very scaly. I don't want to know! Parents' secrets belong to them. Sure there have been times when I was curious about their private life, but I am glad not to know. It's not my business.

"None of us will recover from this for a long while," she says softly, "and for you it will be hardest. I just want you to remember that you are dearly loved and valued. You are a child we are both very proud of, and you are absolutely innocent in all of this. The best part of all these years of marriage, David, is you. The very best, most wonderful part."

"But still not good enough to keep you together?"

"Would you want that?"

"Yes!" I say. "Yes! I want a whole family at least till I'm finished with school and out of the house."

"It used to be," she says, "that sometimes people who hated one another were locked together for life."

"But you and Dad don't hate each other."

What she says next is the saddest thing I have ever heard. "No, we don't hate each other. But we don't love each other enough."

I close my eyes on the pale rim of her mouth

erupting white smoke like a volcano. "Why did he have to take off just before Christmas?" It seems to me, somehow, particularly cruel.

"There would never be a *good* time," she says, "but I understand how you feel. He said he just couldn't pretend any longer."

I make a face to show what I think of that. "What will we do about the tree, Mom?"

"We'll put it up. Life has to continue and Christmas is part of it."

I agree but inside my head my angry mind roars: NO, NO, NO! I have to get out of there. "May I be excused, Mom?"

"Of course. And Dave, don't worry about my smoking. It's temporary. It helps me a bit, gives me something to do with my hands when I want to claw the air."

"Maybe you should look for better help than Marlboros, Mom," I mumble. "Professional help. A shrink or a counselor—something like that."

She looks straight at me. Her lower lip is quivering again, but she's in control. "I'm going to need some privacy and some time, Dave, to work all this out in my own mind. Without outside help. Without any intermediary. Silently. The way I was brought up to do. But if you think you'd like to go to someone for help, son, I—"

"No. I wasn't talking about me. I can handle it."

She nods. "Please bear with me." It's almost a whisper. "Try to be strong yourself and have faith in God."

"I'll try," I say, and I mean it. I realize that she is looking for her own way, off by herself. I am for the first time in my life to be all alone.

*   *   *

We put up the tree in the living room near the fireplace. It's one of those tall skinny trees and Mom decorates it with tiny bells and the porcelain ornaments she's saved from her own childhood: fat-faced Kewpie dolls and elves and small animals. I climb to the top of the ladder and fasten the star. No problem. Who needs a father? We're managing fine. I trip and bang my shin coming down. It's agony.

I need a father!

I suppose it is a pretty tree. I can't stand to look at it and the scent bothers me, so I get out of there as soon as I can. Under it are several packages for me and my tiny package for Mom: a Navaho turquoise and silver ring, which I bought at a garage sale. It wasn't expensive and the blue stone is pretty. Mom took off her rings right after Dad left and there's a band of whiteness on her finger that makes me sad. I can't help staring at it. I keep thinking of Achilles' heel, the one weak spot on the warrior.

A gigantic carton arrives via UPS for me, and Mom stands it behind the couch. I can tell it's a bike. I peek at the tags. A Motobecane. I've been dreaming of this bike practically forever. Well, he can stuff it. I'm not riding any bike he sends. Who would? With his record of reliability? Any bike from him wouldn't steer straight. He really has his nerve; he takes a vanishing powder and then he sends a present. The truly invisible Santa. That's a laugh; he's up at the North Pole.

Christmas morning. Mom loves the Navaho ring, really loves it, not just says so. I can tell. She slips it on and it fits and more than covers the old rings' space. Then she hugs me and hugs me. I get the newest *Guinness Olympic Record Book* and two Talking Heads albums. She must have researched Bean. These are the right presents.

"Send the bike back," I tell her.

"You wanted it very much."

"Not now."

"Wait a bit, Dave, and see."

"I don't want it. Did he send you a conscience present, too?"

"No."

"Well, you're the one he really blasted. You keep the bike."

I have hurt her terribly. "Sorry," I say. "Please send it back, Mom."

She moves her head once in agreement.

Wipe my father out of my life like chalk from a blackboard?

Fat chance.

He lives in my head morning, noon, and night.

He's like that Scottish noble, Macbeth, who murdered sleep. I can't manage more than two, three hours at a time without waking scared and shivering. Me, who sleeps eight hours regularly, ten during the basketball season.

I go through my robot period. I do whatever I am supposed to do, but I do it mechanically and I don't remember any of it. I betray old hydrophobic smelly Queen Isabella; I get up early and I shower. Mom doesn't even notice this major concession. I bring in the *Times* and strip it (it comes in blue plastic) and leave it at Mom's bedroom door; I shake out a bowl of Cheerios or Cap'n Crunch and pour the milk. I remember to drink my juice. I speak when spoken to. I live. Once in a while I am amazed at how smoothly the world keeps moving along without even a bump over the huge pothole in my life.

For the first couple of days A.A. (After Alaska), I am not hungry. The idea of food makes me nauseous, and I have to go hide if there are cooking smells around. I don't eat and Mom doesn't bug me. Soon enough I start eating again, and then I begin pigging out. I stuff my mouth with junk food constantly: Fritos, chocolate chip cookies, pretzels. I crunch thousands of peppermint Christmas candies like they were Life Savers. I also crunch Life Savers. When I'm not eating I'm chewing and popping Hubba Bubba Fruit Gum. Mom doesn't even notice the popping, something she absolutely hates. It's as if she doesn't hear the outside world.

I begin to study her facial expressions, hoping somehow that I'll pick up some of them. People who live together are supposed to grow to look alike. I'd prefer to look like her. Eagerly I scan my face daily in the mirror for signs that I'm getting to frown like Mom, show interest like Mom, smile like her, but there's not a trace. His face looks back at me. I decide to let my hair grow longer. I start a mustache. It comes out reddish brown. Bean says it looks like toast crumbs left over from breakfast. It grows, but slow, very slow. I do look a little less like him, the all-American, clean-shaven, short-haired male. Why couldn't I have Mom's coloring? Why couldn't I resemble her since she's to be my lifetime parent? It's a dirty trick to stick me with a face that reminds me of betrayal. Will my kids look like him, too? What a farce!

Nighttime is Total Terror Time. My dreams are so scary I stay awake as long as possible. I squirm down way under the covers in the dark and lie on the edge of the mattress ready for instant escape. And I sweat! The same hideous nightmare flickers on and repeats itself night after night for weeks.

Even now—a year later—when I close my eyes there is still an occasional replay like an old video: It is a perfectly mellow sweet spring day, one of those green bright days when the world is good.

I am hiking in the fields with my dad. We have had a long, wonderful walk and I am helping him collect mushrooms. He has been teaching me about them for years. He knows which are edible.

He's way up ahead almost at the end of this pasture and into the surrounding pine woods. "Here's a mob of *Agaricus campestris*. A beautiful clump. Not exotic but perfect for tonight's steak."

Agaricus campestris is the common variety of mushroom. In a way I am happiest when he finds those. The rarer ones are dangerous. Once or twice he's made a mistake; he tastes the doubtfuls first; and he's gotten sick. Mom calls it "mushroom macho." That makes him mad.

"Coming," I answer, and I start toward him, but as I walk I see a gigantic pine begin to tilt. It falls in slow motion. I put my head back and watch it come down. I open my mouth to scream. My throat is so clogged I cannot make a sound. The massive tree falls right on him with a thunderous crash. The foliage shudders and he is gone. That's when I wake up and have to gallop to the bathroom. My kidneys always rev up at horror flicks.

No one, not even Bean, knows about this dream. Why don't I call out and warn my father? Why do I feel so guilty all the time: about him and Laurie and Mom and everything? Maybe I don't warn him because I think he deserves what he gets.

I don't believe that. I don't want him to die. I only want him to come back and be what he's supposed to be: my father.

From the moment he goes, Mom is amazingly silent. She never cries when I'm around, but those gray eyes are swollen, the lids puffy. She always looks as if she's about to cry. During winter break she goes on doing what she did before: run the house, volunteer at the library, and take care of me. Her library schedule is very busy because in the children's room there are special holiday hours and a Christmas party. We (I actually help her) bake a hundred large sugar cookies for that event—and twenty-five extra for me.

She has erratic bursts of energy. One night, just as I am going off to listen to music in my room, she suggests that we get rid of Dad's left-behind stuff, clothes and personal junk. "You can keep anything you want," she offers.

"I don't want a thing."

"Then let's do it," she says, and we take huge black plastic leaf bags and go to his closet and take every single thing out and fold it up and place it in the plastic. He left a lot of stuff, but we do a thorough job. I try not to pay attention to the clothes, especially the hiking stuff, because it reminds me of happy times and that hurts. We put his big clumpy old shoes in a carton. Done, just before midnight. Goodwill gets the stuff a few days later.

Mom gets a few invitations to go out, but she won't go to dinner anymore with the couples who were their friends. She finds it awkward. One or two of the wives come around some afternoons and sit in the living room and talk. They shut up when I come in and they look incredibly cheerful. They talk to me real slow and loud. I itch to tell them that when your father deserts you that doesn't cancel your IQ. They behave as if I am some mutant. "How are you now, David?" "You look like you're putting on a little weight, David." "Where did you get those long fingers from, David?" "Those are huge sneakers, David, what size feet do you have?" I get the idea of printing up a card with all my various measurements with maybe one or two exaggerated to shock them, but they are Mom's friends. I let it go. I'm glad she has someone talking to her. She's so silent. They're more Dad's friends, I guess. The charmer. They drop Mom soon enough when she doesn't respond.

She and I, after that first talk, don't discuss *it*. We function like normal people, but a crater has been blasted in the middle of our lives and we tiptoe around it very carefully.

"What would you think—" she starts suddenly out of her silence one morning, "if I changed my name back to Anna? Anna Schlegel Smith."

"Fine, Mom. You can even drop the Smith as far as I'm concerned."

"No. That's a part of my life. But I am really Anna."

"I didn't know that. Why did you shorten it?"

"I got talked into it," she says, her tone scornful of herself.

I don't ask by whom. She goes right out and buys a new nameplate with her old name on it and my name on it too, and she fastens it to the mailbox immediately, and then she subsides.

"You are the man of the house," she says to me another morning after I've killed myself shoveling snow. She means it as a compliment to my hard work but I hate it. I am sixteen years old.

Sixteen years old is not ready yet to be the man of the house.

Thank God for Bean. I would go bananas except for him. One thing I learned from this experience (Am I really saying this? I promised myself I would never say "One thing I learned from this experience . . ." because it is the way adults rub it in when you goof): a good friend, a person who really cares about what happens to you, is the most important thing in life.

Bean and I work it over and over.

"You say this Laurie is really a looker."

"Yeah. In a Playboy bunny kind of way. Big boobs."

"But your mother is good-looking. She's classy."

"My father likes late models. You know he trades his car in every year."

"You say this Laurie is young?"

"Yeah."

Bean scratches his nose. "Then it must be a sexual obsession."

"Genius. You worked that out all alone?"

"All right, if you're so smart. You tell me."

"I can't. I just don't believe that could be all there is to it."

Bean shrugs. "I'm not sure. But it seems to come into a person's head and he can't get rid of it. He can't think of anything else. He's *possessed* the way I used to be about Milky Ways. That's why I traded you my whole full Halloween shopping bag full of candy for all your Milky Ways that time. Remember? When we were ten?"

"I remember. Twenty-seven miniature Milky Ways."

"And I ate them all while you watched."

"Uh. Gross."

"Well, sex seems to grab people the same way. Like in that movie classic they showed in English class, *Wuthering Heights*. That guy Heathcliff was a basket case because of Cathy."

"That guy Heathcliff was a loser from the beginning. His elevator never went all the way to the top. My father is not like him. He's a winner. He's shrewd and cool. He knows how to think things out; that's part of being an engineer."

"Your father is not cool. He is *hot*," Bean says evilly, and he takes off. I chase after him glad of the release. We have open land along the edge of town and we often run there. We race till we're tired; then we walk along and argue.

"I understand about the birds and the bees," I tell him. "What I don't understand is how he can pull such a double-cross on my mother, let alone me."

"Possessed," says Bean mysteriously. "Out of control. You've got to think of your father as some sick guy who can't help himself. Like some druggie who needs his fix. Laurie is your father's fix." He seems to be fascinated with this theory.

I don't want to hear it. In my head I am wondering: And after Laurie will he need another one? Will I grow up like him?

I wish I didn't care. I try hard but, still, I care.

[Attention Admissions Officer: I am trying to tell my story as quickly as I can, but I am afraid of leaving out something important. Please understand.]

Winter recess limps along. I'm glad I don't have to face all the kids in school right off. I wake up early, sometimes at four A.M., so the days are endless. I keep my headphones under my pillow so that when I wake I can just slip them on. I listen to music for hours and hours. When my mother is at home she is usually sitting upstairs in their/her bedroom. She says she is doing a lot of reading and thinking, but what she's doing a lot of is suffering. Bean is around some and that's good, but he's busy with church and chores so he doesn't have too much time.

Afternoons, I walk out a lot by myself along the edge of town. I bundle up against the cold and even wear a hat. (Thirty percent of body heat is lost through the head; fact courtesy Bean.) The snowplows keep the roads clean; mostly I have the snowy meadowlands to myself. An occasional dog-walker and his dog meet me, and sometimes I come across a bunch of happy kids with sleds. I look at them and I envy them; I'd love to be like them, sledding in the crisp snow. The Big Man and I used to race bellywhopping long ago. It didn't matter that he won; it was always fun. Once I heard a whispered argument between my parents. Mom wanted him to let me win, to fix the race. And he wouldn't. "The boy's got to learn to compete," he said. "It's a tough world."

"Not where there's love," she answered.

He laughed and picked up his sled for a running start, and I agreed with him. I never did get to beat him. We stopped racing before I was full-grown.

Mostly no one is out walking, and I can tramp along in the crusty snow arguing with my father in my head.

Why'd you go and do it, Dad?

I can't really explain it.

You have to. You're always telling me a man has to know what he's doing.

You're still a kid. I can't—

I'll bet I know why you can't.

You do?

It's sex, isn't it?

(Slow response.) *That's part of it, yes.*

A big part of it. (I accuse.)

Yes.

The thing I can't forgive most is that you had to make a choice. And you chose her. You could have chosen us. And you chose her!

I couldn't—

Stuff it. I don't want to hear it.

This brilliant conversation with variations is rehearsed over and over in my head.

One bitter cold day I am going along, my hand scrunching a good-sized snowball, and I see Riley Rogers approaching. I'm surprised. At first we both stop, two rigid figures in a winter landscape. I throw the snowball at the high branches of a bare tree near her and it's a face-off. "Hi, David," she begins, hopping over the icy ditch as if it's a normal occurrence for her to be out there on the New Jersey tundra. "How are you?" she asks, her face pink from the cold. She is the lady in red: red parka, red knit gloves and a matching hat. She looks pretty.

41

"Okay," I say.

"Want company?"

"It's a free country."

"That why they call you Mr. Hospitable?" She wheels to go back.

"No—wait—Riley. I'm sorry. It's just that I'm surprised to see you here. Usually there's no one out here but me."

"Your turf," she says. "I'll go. No hard feelings."

"No, really. I don't mind."

She's uncertain.

"I'm glad you came," I say, amazing myself.

"Okay."

We move along side by side in the flat white landscape. The crunch of our boots on the snow breaks the afternoon stillness.

"It's nice out here," Riley says, "as if we were on a holiday from other people."

"Uh huh." These flatlands are one big marsh between the towns. The ground is too mushy for heavy construction so they leave the place alone. Springtime it's all small creeks and runny mud, summer it's grassy, and winter it's a glacier. Like Alaska, where he is, I think to myself. *Why am I doing what he's doing?* I don't want to copy him. But where else can I walk? There are no palm trees and sandy white beaches in northern New Jersey.

"I'm sorry about your father," Riley says, and I stumble and almost go down on the ice. She grabs my arm and steadies me.

"Bean promised—"

"I know. I guessed it before he told me. This is a small town and no one's seen your dad around all vacation. I hope I'm your friend, too. You looked so awful that evening in my house. Like there'd been a death." She stops walking and turns to face me.

42

"That was how I felt. I didn't know it showed."

"It shows to people who like you." She looks down at her boot digging a crack in the snow. "Why do you care that I know? It's no disgrace."

"Yes, it is." I'm having trouble with my voice. It's coming out too high. "To me it is."

We walk on again, quickly.

"David, I'm sorry about your father. But to tell the truth that's not why I'm out here walking today. I've got a problem of my own and I had to get out of the house." Her voice softens. "I could use some advice."

I hardly hear the last line, or I can't believe I heard right. She has faded off.

"You've certainly come to the right person," I say sarcastically. "Dave the fortuneteller. Dave the prophet. Like that Greek guy Teiresias in that crazy play. I'm blinder than he was. I couldn't see what was happening under my own nose."

She goes on talking as if she didn't hear me, but I've come to understand that kind of deafness. Misery has a way of cutting you off so you don't really connect with anyone else. Like you're tuned into a Walkman that plays only your own troubles. Mom's like that these days. And, I suppose, me. And now Riley is listening only to Riley.

"I'm having a hard time," she says, "with my mother. You know how I love to sing? Well, it's fine with her as long as it's church choir and school chorus. But I want to write my own songs. I want to try doing popular music, so I went ahead and joined Rockabye—the new pop music group that's forming—and Mom is upset. She wants me to quit."

I nearly flip at that. Riley is the All-American good girl. Bean complains all the time that he gets

43

(himself) into hot water and she never does. She is also implying that her mother is unreasonable. But Mrs. Rogers is an incredibly calm, logical person. "I always thought your mother was about as fair as a mother could be."

"That's what makes it so hard. She is fair about most things. But she's a fanatic about popular music. She's seen a couple of videos and she hates the whole scene: the music itself, the loudness, the singers' clothes, the punks, the drugs, and the dirty meanings. She has a long list of indictments, like a prosecutor. And she just can't believe that there are some great songs."

For the first time since David, Sr., drove off with his Eskimo Pie, I stop being miserable for myself, alone. I feel sorry for Riley. She has a high, sweet voice and since grade school she's been a part of school musical programs. No concert is ever held without Riley Rogers doing a solo.

"How can I advise you, Riley? I'm up at bat with two broken arms. I've got to heal so I can function."

"You can listen, anyway. They say psychiatrists are nutty with all kinds of personal problems— that's why they choose the field—but they listen and help others worse off."

That one makes me laugh. "Sure, I'll listen. But don't put any money on my solutions. Doctor David Smith is a quack."

She grins at me. "You're making me feel better already." She digs out tissues and blows her nose, a loud healthy blast, the blow of a woman with a good psychiatrist. "Excuse me. I'm ready now. The way I see it I have two choices: I can do what Mom wants me to do, quit Rockabye; or I can hang in there and cause trouble at home."

"Or she can make you quit."

"She would never do that. She leaves it up to me and it's much harder that way. The pressure is on me."

"How about your father?"

"He goes along. He respects her judgment."

We reach a turn in the path and go round a giant tree with gnarled branches and twig fingers reaching up, and we start back while I am thinking it over. I try to pass. I don't have the brains for such a serious decision for Riley.

"You need a wiser man than me for this, Riley. A King Solomon kind of mind with a keen sense of judgment."

"Huh. He wasn't so wise. I hate that story. They tell it all the time in Sunday School, and when I was younger I used to be frightened by it. What if, when he was trying to decide who the baby belonged to, neither mother had spoken up? What if the true mother was scared speechless? What if she had laryngitis that day? He'd have a sliced baby on his hands."

"Gross," I say.

"I'll tell you which way I'm tending," she says. "I'm thinking of giving in."

"Why?"

"It's my personality, I guess. I don't like to make trouble."

"Who likes to make trouble?" I ask her. "That's not the point. Be honest with yourself. If singing in Rockabye is important to you, fight for it."

She's uncertain. "The problem is trying to decide how important it is."

"I guess one way is thinking about how much you'll miss it if you quit."

"Mmm." She looks up at the gray sky. "What would you do?"

So I end up giving her advice. I don't mean to, but I see how bad she wants to go that way and I help her a little. "If I loved to sing as much as you do, I think I would fight for it. It's as if someone said to me, 'No more basketball'; I sure wouldn't let it go easy, I'm telling you."

"Thanks, David."

"You can call me Dave."

She's pleased. "Okay, Dave. Want to stop at my house for a hot chocolate?"

"Over my dead body."

"Offer withdrawn."

"Uh . . . uh, Riley." I am the king of clumsiness. It seems as if I can't say two words without having to go back and explain myself. "I didn't mean it like it sounded. I was drinking hot chocolate when Mom broke the news to me and I barfed it all up. So I'm off the stuff. I'll never touch another drop. You are looking at the founder of Hot Chocolates Anonymous."

She scoops up a fistful of snow. "You are a bit of a nerd," she says, and showers me. She doesn't pack it right for a snowball so it's all powder. She's gone before I can demonstrate how to pack snow.

A bit of a nerd. Not an altogether hundred percent nerd. That is the nicest personal thing any girl has ever said to me.

We walk again, Riley and I, during the winter break. I look out for her each day as I turn off the main road onto the flats. If she's not there I move along real slow for a while so she can catch up if she's coming. When she doesn't show, I'm disappointed.

46

Then I get mad at myself because I used to enjoy walking alone, before. Now, I'm lonely.

I decide to tell her about it one afternoon. "I like walking with you, Riley, but I wish I didn't."

"Thanks." She laughs at me.

"I mean I'd rather be completely independent, so I never end up like Mom. Her life got too mixed-up with mine and Dad's. We ate steak and potatoes, and burgers, and fried chicken to suit Dad. Spaghetti was the only foreign dish he liked. And pizza. Even though she cuts out recipes for the weirdest things, she never tried them. She didn't work at a real job—to suit him. Even her name, Anna, got cut down to Ann because he thought it sounded better. It was as if nothing she preferred was important enough or worth the fuss." Suddenly I make a connection in my head. "In many ways it's like you, Riley, thinking that joining Rockabye isn't worth the fuss for you. Look what happened to Mom. When he walked out she was left with little pieces of herself like a jigsaw puzzle. She's got nothing to travel with now till she puts herself back together."

Riley understands. "Still,—" she says, "—completely independent is too lonely. For people it's wrong."

Makes sense. Some kind of balance is what's needed. How come my mother who's very smart didn't know that? What happened to her life?

Once in a while Bean walks with us. One afternoon we three build the most overweight snowman of the century: Mr. Elvis the Pelvis, round and hard-packed with a zucchini nose and shades (a pair Bean contributes from his glamorous period when he was fourteen). Riley gives Mr. Elvis Magic Marker sideburns and he is a scream. He stands for three cold weeks and we salute him when we pass:

> I don't want to be your tiger
> Because tigers play too rough
> I don't want to be your lion
> Because lions ain't the kind you love enough
> I just want to be your teddy bear
> Put a chain around my neck and lead me anywhere
> Oh let me be your teddy bear . . .

I am finding it easier to talk to Riley about almost anything while we are out there walking. Much easier than it would ever be at a party or in some room where other people are watching and every time I make a move I bump into a chair or knock something over.

"Listen," Bean grabs me alone one afternoon, "what's with you and my clone Riley?"

"Nothing. We're friends."

He doesn't look all that enthusiastic. We've been buddies so long I can pretty much tell what he's thinking. He liked it better without Riley.

"Okay, I give my consent," he says.

"Nobody asked you."

"I give it anyway." He sees I'm getting sore. "Listen, banana, I'm one of those weirdos who cares about his friends. My kid sister"—born three minutes after him—"is a pest, but she is better than most girls. She's straight with you. So, I inquire. And I approve. For friendship. Definitely not for marriage."

"No one will ever marry her," I say sadly, "because he'd get you for a brother-in-law."

He loves that.

"Do me a favor," I ask. "Don't tell her we talked about her."

"What am I, stupid?"

"A rhetorical question," I say wisely, "requires no response. The assumption is that only one answer is possible."

He rewards me with a really amazing razz. Bean could substitute for a tuba in a brass band. The man has talent.

Mrs. Rogers does not discuss Rockabye with Riley. Once Riley decides she is going to stay in it, Mrs. R. withdraws. "You do what you want. Just see your grades don't suffer and your chores get done. I don't want to hear about it."

Riley agrees.

"And no practicing in this house when I am at home, please."

So, on the surface things are okay. But Riley is unhappy. "Things aren't the same," she tries to explain to me, "because I never quarrelled with Mom about anything major before. Small things we could argue about and negotiate. But now it's like there's been a break in our family and a repair job; invisible glue fills the cracks so they can't be seen, but they are there. The cracks are in our minds, in our memories; we know where the glue is holding the break together."

She looks so sad I put my arms around her and hug her close to me. It seems a natural and nice thing to do, nice for me, too. I don't tell her she's lucky to have all the parts glued. My life is a pile of shards. Hugging her feels so good I don't let up for a while.

It could become a habit.

To keep the record straight, David Smith, Sr., is a man of his word about money. It's part of his ethos: a man pays his debts. He sends a check to start the new year. In fact, *two* pale blue envelopes appear, and the bulkier one has my name on it. I leave it there on the hall shelf, unopened, hoping it will disappear, get lost, blow away, fall behind the radiator, disintegrate. I can't bear to look at it as I pass through the front hall, yet I look to see it each time.

"There's a letter to you from him," Mom says after several days. She speaks of Dad only that way now: "he" or "him"; she avoids mentioning his name or his relationship to us.

"I know. I saw it."

"What will you do about it?"

"I don't know."

"You'll have to do something."

"I know."

"David?"

"I can't decide if I should tear it up, burn it, or send it back to him."

"If you don't want any mail from him then I think you should send it back. That way he'll know. Maybe he won't write again."

I take her advice. I print "RETURN TO SENDER" in red ink on both front and back. Then I, per-

50

sonally, carry it to the post office and mail it. The clerk assures me that he'll have it in three or four days. I dust off my hands. Mission accomplished. That's what *I* think. Next month the conscience fund arrives again in its thin airmail envelope, and, again, a second identical envelope is there addressed to me. I turn mine around and send it back that very day, but I understand. The Big Man is used to making the rules. He's a winner and you don't say no to a winner. He doesn't hear it easy, anyway. I dread the beginning of the month and those envelopes with the neatly typed addresses. Does she do his typing for him? *Oh, let's write a letter to our son!* I hate the envelopes with the money in them, as well, but he was right. We need the money to live on.

During the first weeks of the new term I can hardly bring myself to go to school at all. When I do go, I doze off in class. I seem to be able to sleep better in noisy, light places than in the quiet darkness of my bedroom. It feels safer. I try keeping the light on and running the stereo in my room, but that doesn't work. I can't figure it. I never dozed off in a public place before, not even on a bus.

Sleeping in school is not really safe. Teachers take it personally when you sleep in their classes. Several times I get sent to the guidance office with a pink slip. The counselor looks me over cautiously for signs of drugs. When he sees I'm clean he wants to know if I'd like "help." The school shrink would be glad to . . .

I'm horrified at the idea of some unknown bozo chewing over the juicy morsels of my life. "No, thank you," I say. "I'm having a little insomnia problem, but I'm sure I can solve it."

51

The pink slip goes into the file and I return to class, only to doze off again another day.

My father's going away blew my thinking fuses. Overload and complete burnout. Even when I drag myself to school and shuffle along through the corridors, avoiding the other members of the basketball team whenever I catch sight of them, I just wait it out, wait for the bell to blast us out of the room and move us on to the next one.

I'm dead. I'm a sixteen-year-old zombie. How do I know I'm dead? I don't even notice girls any more.

My usual pastime was to spend a lot of time scanning them in their tight jeans and bright sweaters, lovely curves, sleeves bunched up to show their arms, their hair all curled and shining or punky or shellacked into place. I liked to smell their perfumes and cosmetics mixed in with chalk. I liked to see their lips glistening with lipstick. I liked to look even though I didn't own.

At my age my father had a steady girl, Frances, stacked but brainless. Stacked was what counted in Oak Park. A cheerleader. I understand that.

Nothing penetrates the murkiness. Books, lessons, girls are remote, irrelevant. The stimuli do not go past the eyes or ears and into the head. This must be what it is like to be retarded. You try desperately to hang on to ideas or even words, but they tease you and disappear. It's frustrating.

What do Tsar Nicholas and Rasputin and Sarajevo and Woodrow Wilson have to do with David Smith, Jr., of Cloverdale, New Jersey? (I must do something about my name. I HATE IT!) How do tangents of curves or arithmetic variables or irregular French verbs relate to my father's unfaithfulness? Because *that* is what I care about. *All* I care about.

"You're obsessed," Riley tells me sadly. "I understand why but you are definitely obsessed."

I nod. She spends a lot of time with me and she's been very patient. It must be so boring for her that I can only deal with this one thing over and over. His departure was a deep scratch in the record of my life, and I'm stuck there and can't move on. "I am obsessed," I admit. "What happened between my father and me is betrayal. The person I admired most and counted on most let me down."

"I know," she says wearily.

"What a humungous mistake I made. I thought because we lived in the same house we were close."

"You've said it all before, Dave. Many, many times. It doesn't do any good to go over it and over it. You just make yourself suffer."

"That's what obsession means, Riley. You called it right."

She says the first unkind thing I ever heard from her. "Don't get to enjoy chewing over your misery. It's not a healthy diet."

"I'm trying," I say. "Honest, I'm trying. I'm not enjoying it a bit."

But I am unable to help myself. Here I am, sixteen years old, growing so fast my legs block the aisle (when Bean sits next to me in class we take up practically the whole last row), almost a man but not yet if being a man means being able to climb right up after a knockdown. I'm not up. I'm on my knees scrabbling around for the ropes to hoist myself.

I am my mother's son. She sits inert in her bedroom or in the living room, the draperies closed so that no crack of sunlight enters. She says she is reading, and sometimes there is an open book on her lap, but she is not. She is feeling her own pain privately. Guess who else is not reading? Mom notices and she feels sorry for me. She reminds me gently, again and again, "David, school is important and you're so good at it. You should go to school."

"I will," I promise her. "I will. Just give me a little time for recovery."

She understands, but she persists. I know she doesn't like to bug me. I keep promising, and each time I really mean it.

The school's got this attendance system. If you're there for homeroom, you're present for the day. If you're not there, the nurse phones home. When the nurse calls, Mom tells her I am not well. She's covering for me, but she's not really lying because I feel terrible. I am too depressed to pretend. I am too depressed to show up for homeroom and then duck out of individual classes in the many ways that are possible. My grades start on a downhill spiral that is awesome. Whenever I do show in school some conscientious teacher calls me up to the desk to talk to me and to recommend tutoring. My teachers think I can catch up. They encourage me. They say they're concerned about me.

I reassure them all. Yes, yes, I can catch up on my own. I'm just having a few hard months. Junior slump.

Actually, I couldn't care less.

What saves me is that I was doing okay before the Christmas break so the teachers carry me through with C's and C-'s; nobody fails you for sickness and my mom reports me sick. It's true. I hardly sleep.

I cut classes heavily early in the term. In a

54

regional high school like ours classes are large and students can stay mostly anonymous. There are ways to slip out. So I slip.

I am killing myself as far as basketball is concerned. Bean begs me to come. "We didn't have a whole season last year because you and your folks took off for D.C. Okay. You've got to do it this term and get your letter."

I don't answer.

"Dave, you don't have to punish yourself. Your father deserves it, not you."

"Quit the amateur psychology," I warn him, but I know he is right. Deep down I don't feel I deserve to do what I love to do most—play basketball. Deep down I enjoy hurting and I want to hurt more. "I don't want to hear about the team or basketball," I tell Bean. "I'm not interested." I refuse to discuss it further. He's baffled.

There is nothing in my whole life that I would rather do than play basketball: dribble down the court and sink an easy shot, or intercept, or take a pass and handle it brilliantly, or take a quick bearing in a crisis and heave a clean shot. On the basketball court I am fluid; intuition and intelligence and body flow together as they do nowhere else. Normally, I'm a bit of a klutz; I say the wrong things and my body finds objects to bump against. On the basketball court people applaud me. Me, David Smith, Jr. Applause kisses my ears and catapults me upward.

I want to play basketball but I can't help myself. In order to play you need to practice. Practice is after school and you're not permitted to attend if you didn't show in your classes. Rules of the school. Mostly I can't drag myself to the building so I end up out all day. It was so easy to tell Riley what to do compared with telling myself.

I know what's coming. It has to come. I feel it on its way. I don't help myself. I'm dying and I don't help myself.

It comes.

Bean brings me the bad news. I think he feels worse than I do, if that's possible, because we two have played together whenever my father's jobs kept us here in Cloverdale. Playing together is only a small part of it. Basketball is fooling around in the locker room, traveling together on the bus, wearing the school jackets, and laughing at all the different cretins we meet. Basketball is suspense and triumph and failure; it's a way of life and it's my way of life and I let it go. I punish myself. Hard.

Bean is really broken up. "Celantano says he's sorry. You're not reliable. You're a good man but he's got to have players who are there every school day. You can't stay on the team if you don't make daily practice."

"Yeah," I say.

"If you came in tomorrow and swore you'd be there regularly, he might change his mind, Dave."

"I can't. I'd be lying. I'm not into school just now."

"What are you into?"

"I wish I knew. Don't hassle me, Bean."

He nods.

It was on the basketball court that the Alaskan runaway loved me best. He was my number one fan and I played like crazy for him. He would yell himself hoarse so he wouldn't have any voice left each time. I could hear him over the crowd, I swear I could. "Davy, Davy, Davy boy. Up. Davy boy, up, up. In!" Afterward, Mom would warm

Dole pineapple juice for him to drink to soothe his throat. He hated the taste so he used to make ridiculous faces, but he always said it was worth it. Then he went away and he took it all with him. I just can't make it now. Part of me wants to, but a bigger part of me wants to spite him. Boy, would it hurt him if he knew. That's pretty peculiar, because he doesn't know. So who does it hurt? Me. More than anyone would believe. It's all so complicated. My mother, the warmest, most loving person I know, sits frozen in the half-light like a princess under a spell. And Dave, her son, can't do a simple thing like get himself out of bed and to school on time. We are suffering from a disease: rejection paralysis.

Bean chatters to cover up how lousy he feels. "Celantano is so hungry to win he's amazing. Today he taped up a big sign in the shower room: 'Show me a good and gracious loser and I'll show you a failure.'"

"Sounds like Woody Hayes," I guess. "Stresses sportsmanship."

"Knute Rockne."

"Could've been Woody Hayes, easy."

The two of us sit silently and contemplate Celantano's madness. Short, barrel-bellied, with a bullet head, the man needs to win in basketball more than he needs to breathe. The tragedy of his life is that he's built for the wrong sport. He'd be a great wrestler, but he fell in love with the hoops.

Bean taps the floor with his big foot for a while. "You're not dropping out of school, are you, Dave?"

"No. I don't know what I'm doing. I just can't hack it every day. When I do come in I feel as if my jacket says NO FATHER; when I walk into a class and they all look at me I think they're thinking *David's father took off with a fox.*"

"That's crazy. There are three thousand kids in this school from six different towns. They don't know what happened in your house. And, besides, it happens in their houses, too. Half of them, maybe more, live with single parents."

"That doesn't make it easier. I'm sorry for all of them. I can't connect with anything the teachers are saying, Bean. It's as if they're talking to me over broken telephones. Nothing comes over that makes sense or seems meaningful, like I ought to remember it."

"I think you're suffering from shock," Bean says. "Either that or you've got some rare form of juvenile senility." This diagnosis breaks us both up. When we recover Bean says to me, "I'm waiting for you to come back to the world full-time, Dave. Being on the team without you is going to be lousy. But we can still play pick-up games. I need you around because you make me look good. You're such a crummy shot."

I punch his shoulder and promise to give it a try.

I've got to break it to the lady of the house, and I don't want it to be a major production. This takes some doing. I get her while she's opening the mail.

"By the way, I'm not playing basketball anymore, Mom," I tell her, real casual. "I just don't have the time for it."

She drops the letters she's holding, and we both bend to pick them up. "I'm sorry, son," she says, while we're still bending over so we don't suffer into each other's face. "I am so sorry."

Ironic. It's letter day; two of the letters are his airmail specials.

"No sweat," I tell her, putting the junk mail in her hands.

She is a lady. She takes those hateful envelopes and leaves it at that.

On the days I don't go to school I still wake very early, but I lie there till I go back to sleep and I sleep till twelve or one. Then I shower, sometimes, and I eat whatever I can find that's easy: salami and cheese sandwiches or chunky Skippy; cold leftovers, anything. I know how to make omelets and pancakes but I don't bother. *He* taught me how. (I've picked up Mom's habit of avoiding his name.) Those two dishes, barbecued chicken and burgers and steak, are *his* dishes, and boy, he could do a job cooking them. Mom always did everything else. It's funny what a fuss we made over his cooking. I never wondered about it before; didn't she mind?

I actually asked her about it. She smiled that remote little smile that meant long distance from where we were. "When he cooked," she said, "it was surprising. A little like Dr. Johnson's dog walking on his hind legs; the wonder was that he was doing it at all. At first, everything he made was terrible. But he did learn."

"Didn't you mind that he got so many compliments?"

She looked vague. "I suppose I did sometimes. Mostly I was entertained by the novelty: the Big Man in the kitchen."

After I eat and wash the dishes I turn on the TV and watch some idiot game show. Or I listen to my stereo, loud. My room is soundproof so I can turn up the volume and forget there's a damaged

59

world out there. The day passes and I hardly notice. Mom and I have dinner and then there's more TV or more music till I fold. Sometimes I pop some corn and eat it all. Not a bad life. Just sort of purposeless.

I could smoke pot. I could do drugs. Sniffing, swallowing, shooting up; the stuff is all around. How would that help me? What are the smokes doing for Mom? I don't ever want to be captive, not to any person and not to any thing.

So early winter passes. Riley appears one mild winter day when I'm out walking on the flats. "Don't start in on me, Riley," I say. "I know it all already. I ought to be in school."

"I didn't say anything yet."

"But you looked."

"How did I look?"

"Like a girl who was about to say, 'Come to school!' "

"It's your guilty conscience telling you that."

"Maybe. I just can't get myself there, Riley. When I do go and they call 'David Smith,' it's like the real David Smith is on Mars. I'm miserable and I sit there panicked at the possibility that I'll be called on and I'll have to stand up and give an answer, and they'll all know."

"What? What will they know?"

"That something rotten happened in the Smith family."

She shakes her head.

"So I stay away. Let's drop it. What did you come out here for?"

"To tell you to come to school." She takes off and I chase her. She's fast and I'm sort of out of shape so we go a long way before I catch her, panting, her face flushed. "Come to school," she says again. I begin to tickle her under the arms.

"Stop saying that," I order.

She collapses. "Come to school. Come—okay, okay, I swear I'll stop."

I let her recover, my fingers poised and ready to tickle again if she dares. She's so pretty. Suddenly I get a great idea. "I would like to kiss you, Riley," I say.

She's incredibly embarrassed. "Dave—I'm sort of backward. That is—I'm going to wait—till I'm older?" She is absolutely wasted with shyness, looking everywhere but not at me.

I take her chin and turn her face so she is looking at me. She's beautiful, her blue eyes dark and her skin soft and pink. "Dope," I say, "I only want to kiss you. I'm worse than backward, myself. I'm severely retarded when it comes to sex. Having Romeo for a father didn't help me any. I *only* want to kiss you."

"I don't even really know how," she says.

"We'll practice," I promise. We do.

Some things I seem to be able to learn.

[Attention Admissions Officer: I am not bragging here, but I am simply telling the truth. This is one of the few good parts of that truth.]

"Funny," she says, when we are walking back, "Dad warned me not to come out here and disturb you. He says this is your mourning period and a man needs to work things out for himself. But I didn't see why you're so different from me. When I'm in trouble I look for a friend—or Mom—someone. So I came."

I feel tremendously grateful to Mr. Rogers for caring. I didn't think he ever noticed me much.

61

He's always so busy with work and his house and the church. Usually when I see him he's tired. But I am so glad Riley is here.

So glad I break down and tell her about the nightmare. What I couldn't bring myself to tell my best male friend—Bean—I easily confide in Riley. She listens. She doesn't comment on the dream or try to talk me out of my fears. All she says is "I'm going to take the phone into my room every night, Dave, from now on. When it gets tough for you, call me. Don't worry about the time; I'm an instant sleeper. I go back without trouble. Call me whenever. . . ."

I feel gratitude, but much more than that. I can't believe it. I feel joy. Both Riley and Bean like me enough to miss me. Two out of three thousand is not bad. I was never Joe Popularity in any grade. *He* used to worry that I didn't have many friends. "I always had a million buddies," he'd remember. Modest, that's my progenitor. Last time he said it, when I was fifteen, I thought my first disloyal thought about him. I surprised myself. *I guess that's the difference between us,* I thought. Always before I had denied or tried to erase any difference.

Now that I'm in trouble I can just sense the other kids keeping their distance, moving back from trouble. They look right through me: the Invisible Smith. Not Riley and Bean.

I celebrate silently. My friends!

I use my Emergency Hot Line. As Riley promised she would, she carries the telephone up every evening and plugs it in in her room. When things get really hairy, I phone her. She makes a big point about the reverse being true—when she's in trouble she'll call me—but we both know who will do the late-night calling. Riley sleeps like a dinosaur: an average of five rings is needed to wake her. She keeps the phone on her bed next to her pillow.

During the first weeks after we make this Hot Line arrangement I start up three times gasping and shivering from watching the giant pine come down in slow motion and crush the Big Man. Obliterate him. There's not a trace! The ground foliage moves in great rolling curves like a tidal wave. I call Riley and once she's awake, slow and gentle, she talks me back to normal. After each call I manage to sleep, perhaps because I know she's out there ready to listen. In the morning the sheets are all pulled out and sweat-wet, but fitful sleep is possible.

One weird moonless night—snow on the ground pillowing Cloverdale in endless silence—I eat all the peanuts in a twelve ounce Planter's jar while watching two putrid TV movies dealing with divorce. I'm sick of the rotten way people behave toward each other. I smell to myself like an elephant and I can't stand it, the ugliness and the peanut smell and the silence. I pick up my lit book to see what's going on in English class tomorrow. The syllabus lists a contemporary American play, *The Glass Menagerie*, by Tennessee Williams, ". . . to be done aloud in class." Mrs. Aronson, our teacher, is a frustrated thespian (actor or actress; from Thespis, father of Greek tragedy, definition courtesy Dawn Aronson). I open to the first page to check this play out.

It's set in St. Louis. Tom, a merchant seaman is standing alone in a darkened alley, smoking and talking. This will be a reminiscence, he tells us, presenting truth gently as illusion. He mentions the other characters we're going to meet: his mother, Amanda; his sister, Laura; and a gentleman caller. Then Tom begins to go on about a fifth character in the play, his father, who will never appear onstage. Only a large picture of him remains because the man himself skipped out. Last they heard from him, Tom notes bitterly, was a picture postcard from Mexico. It seems he "fell in love with long distances . . ."

I panic. What is happening? Every conversation, and TV program, and lecture, and headline I come across is suddenly dealing with the broken family, desertion, divorce, aid to dependent children. The world is all of a sudden focusing on my problem, pointing its finger in my direction. But that's crazy.

"Riley? It's Dave."

"Yes?" Her voice is faint, sleepy. "You okay?"

"I don't know."

"The nightmare again?"

"No. Worse. I think my mind is going. Paranoia has moved in. This phone call presents truth in the pleasant disguise of humor."

"Dave, you read the play." She's pleased.

"Only the first couple of pages."

"Oh. Tell me what's wrong."

"I think I'm obsessed. Suddenly everything I see or hear about these days deals with divorce. Every TV program, every conversation, every headline is about broken families, fathers pulling out, abuse. I can't get away from it. I just turned off the TV after two movies, both about divorce. Then I looked at our English assignment for tomorrow and there's this play."

A long pause while she considers this. "Dave, what were today's headlines in the *New York Times?*"

"Never read it."

"You should. Let me get the paper. Just a sec."

I wait. Her idea of a second is laughable. She probably has to creep downstairs through the darkened house and find it.

"Here I am. Top headline: 'Russians Say Peace Is Prime Global Objective,'" she reads. "'PLO Refuses to Negotiate with Israel.' 'Famine Increases in the Sahel.' See, Dave, plenty of trouble but not a thing about divorce. You're just hypersensitive to the subject because it's on your mind so much. The topic was around before, but now you hear and see things selectively."

"Never mind the front page. You just look at the family page."

Pages rustling. "Not a thing. The feature today is converting lofts into apartments. Then—let's see—there's a society column and a long piece on how to make your own yogurt. You need milk and a bacteria culture."

"No kidding."

"Listen, Dave, if you're okay I'd like to go back to sleep. I'm reading the part of Laura tomorrow and I want to be good. Come to class and watch. It's a good play."

"I'll see."

"I'll look for you. Please come. I need you in my claque."

"You've got Bean."

"That's a laugh. He said if he had the courage of his convictions he'd come with two pounds of overripe tomatoes."

"Ah, Riley. You'll do fine."

Since I'm up very early, I decide to do the school bit. Turns out *The Glass Menagerie* is a terrific play and Riley breaks everyone's heart as Laura, she's so good. Mrs. Aronson with her frosted blond hair flying and her dark-pencilled eyebrows is a wonderful Amanda Wingfield, the mother in the play, a faded southern belle. I both hate her and admire her.

I despise the father for running away and then rubbing it in.

Mal Harris, a tall blond geek with waxy skin and big ears, hates the play. He's making cracks all through the hour about queers and pansies and how if he was Tennessee Williams's father he'd run, too. I can't hear Laura's speeches because he's running on at the mouth.

"Be quiet," I tell him. "No one wants to hear you."

He gives me the finger.

Sitting in English class, angry, furious, in fact, I forget about principles. I forget about what makes sense. "Outside, afterward," I promise him, "unless you want a go right here, now." I'm no fighter but I'm not afraid. My father bought me gloves

66

(against Mom's wishes) when I was a kid and we used to spar. I've never really tested my skill because Mom's nonviolence always made sense. "As a goal," she argues, "as an ideal to work toward. Sit on your fists and use your mind."

Mal shuts up but the end of the play is spoiled for me; the atmosphere is polluted. I am steaming.

Outside we go at it without a word. I color his left eye and raise a welt on his cheek under it. I guard my face like it's china because I don't want Mom to know about this. She's got enough on her now. So he lands a couple of hard ones in the gut. He gets me once in the mouth and loosens a front tooth. I taste my own blood and hate it, but the rage of months is inside me and I believe I really might have hurt him and him me except that just as we're getting dangerous we get separated by, of all people, Celantano, the basketball coach, on his way to the car park. Celantano has it in for me.

"Ah, Smith. You couldn't show for basketball. You trying to substitute boxing?" His square brutal jaw grins as if he's just made a major joke. He doesn't let us off with a warning; he takes us to the dean's office.

Dean Packard is a rare educational bird. He's black; he has a reputation for being just, and color-blind about students; and he's brief, even stingy, with the words. (That can be said of no other high school official in the United States. Maybe in the world.) At this moment he's busy with the marijuana crowd. I get a contact high just sitting there. Celantano deposits us on the bench (one on either end) and he fills out a statement. Me, he gives the all-time, murder-is-too-good-for-you, you-traitor look because I violated his code. I betrayed basketball. Then he leaves.

Oh Celly Belly, if you only knew what it cost me to drop out of basketball. To be dropped out of basketball. I love it more than you do, if that's possible. There is nothing, *nothing* in this world I would rather do than play—not even have sex, which is the ultimate fantasy for Bean and most of the guys. So don't put me down. It was a necessary sacrifice. My family died this semester, Celly Belly. I couldn't bounce a ball on the fresh grave.

Usually three days' suspension is the penalty for fighting on school grounds. Whoever decided that keeping a kid out of school is punishment must be the all-time marshmallow administrator of the century. I sit there and keep my mouth shut and hope no one will look at my attendance record. I want to be suspended. I lust for it.

While I'm sitting on the bench waiting for Packard, I think about the play and Tennessee Williams and how good Riley was as Laura. Riley thinks a lot about the Lauras of the world, the losers of the world, and she feels sad for them. No matter how down she is, she remembers them. It's an odd quality. Mom, before she was knocked out of the game into silence, had it, too. I sit there remembering Mrs. Aronson's little introductory speech saying the play was highly autobiographical though Tennessee Williams's father never actually ran away. He distanced himself from his son and treated him hatefully. He was a drunkard and a brute, who wouldn't let his son go back for his senior year at college but got him a job in a shoe factory. The playwright writes about his own life, Mrs. Aronson explained, but he changes things. An artist takes his own experience and then invents and leaves out to create his art. She recommended *Remember Me to Tom*, a book by the playwright's mother, for anyone interested. Suddenly, I'm very interested.

Maybe Riley is right. Maybe I am too sensitized to what's happened in my family. Maybe it was going on all along around me before the putrid hot chocolate in the stucco diner: fathers deserting, or dying, or brutalizing, families in trouble. Tennessee Williams sure knew about it more than fifty years ago. He had it hard; you can tell from the play. I'm going to read that book by his mother, and I'm going to look up some other writers I admire and see what their lives were like.

Packard's secretary calls us to go in. If I'm suspended I'm going to use my time investigating all of this.

The dean sits at a huge, neat metal desk. He wears a black suit, white shirt, striped tie. He's a handsome man: dark, stern, thin intelligent face, small mustache. He's too good for Edison Regional; he's *Doctor* Packard. Dignity. The man has it.

Mal Harris and I stand in the dock.

He reads Celantano's note. "Fighting," he says. "Want to tell me about it?"

Neither of us unbuttons.

"Well, what have you two to say for yourselves?"

I keep my peace. Mal begins to beg: his attendance and punctuality are perfect. *He's always prepared in gym class.* This is his first trouble. His father has angina and this will make him much sicker. Mercy. Mercy! He *sirs* the dean to death. He's disgusting.

The dean sends for his records and he sees that he is telling the truth. Reprieve. Detention and a two-month probationary period. A little more grovelling and Mal Harris crawls out.

My turn. "Smith?" Packard says, and waits. "Anything to say for yourself?"

I shake my head.

"Is there some way I can help you—off or on the record?"

One thing I do not want is for him to see my attendance record.

"No, Dean Packard."

He studies me. I stay dumb.

"You leave me no alternative. Three days' suspension. Your parents will be notified."

"Mother," I correct him.

"Smith?"

"My mother will be notified. I haven't got a father—at home." First public acknowledgment. Why did I do it? I wish someone would pull out my tongue. Why did I have to add "at home"?

"Noted." He actually writes it down. Then he looks me over for a minute. "Did this just happen—at home?"

I'm not doing well. I have to get out of there. I don't want his sympathy. Wait a minute, maybe I do want his sympathy, but I don't want to lose my three precious days.

"A while ago," I mumble.

"Want to talk about it?"

"You ever know anyone in my place who wants to talk about it?" I sound more belligerent than I mean to, but he's caught me off-guard.

"Some," he says. "A few. You can always come back if you change your mind. I'd be glad to help. I'm trained in counseling." He actually smiles at me. "I don't only do suspensions."

"Thanks, Dean Packard."

I am dismissed with a wave of his hand.

Triumph! Three days to stay out of school

because they don't want me there. I won't have to skulk around hiding from kids, teachers, Mom. Of course, I still have to explain it to Mom, the suspension and my loose tooth. She probably wouldn't notice the tooth but I'm going to have to eat soft-boiled eggs for a few days; she'll notice that.

I tell Bean about the suspension and my plans to do the reading.

"Man, that's morbid," he says.

"Research." I defend it.

"Morbid. Why don't you look up writers with nice happy families?"

"Name three." He looks at me blank as a baby. "Anyway, that play started me thinking. It said something to me."

"Yeah. Don't work in a shoe factory." He ducks the avenging poke. "You shouldn't have fought Harris," he says. "He's not in your class. He's flyweight above the ears."

"He got to me. You're not going to believe this. He has perfect punctuality, perfect attendance, and a perfect record for being prepared in gym."

Bean loves it, particularly the gym bit. "I believe it, I believe it. He comes every day and he changes his socks. He can't think, but what does that matter? He ought to get an award. A trophy. Bronzed socks!"

I give Bean five for that winning idea.

Telling Mom about it is much harder than talking to Dean Packard.

In the evening I let her light up and puff for a while. I'm sweating and I can't keep my feet still. They start tapping. She notices I'm unstrung. "What's wrong, Dave?"

I break it to her. "I got suspended today for fighting. I'm sorry."

"Fighting?" A dull red colors her pale cheeks. "Who were you fighting with?"

"Some kid. I don't even know him."

"That doesn't make much sense, does it? I've asked you not to use violence, Dave."

"I try. This was the first time and I couldn't help it. He was talking all through English class while they were acting out this play, *The Glass Menagerie*. I couldn't hear. Riley Rogers, Bean's sister, had a part and I couldn't hear her."

Mom is really disturbed. "Was there a teacher present?"

"Sure. She was up front, acting." Mothers are weird. Did she really expect me to raise my hand and tell the teacher Mal was talking? She did, really.

"There were other ways to handle it, I'm sure. You should not have fought."

"Mom—"

"I'm ashamed of you."

"I'm having a hard time in school."

"You hardly go," she says slowly, "and when you do go you fight." With difficulty, she brings her eyes and her mind back and focuses entirely on me. "I know you're having a terrible time. That's why I haven't pressed you to go. That and the fact that I, too, am in trouble. I know I've been remiss in not keeping close to you, but you must forgive me, son." Her body is trembling. "I am slow to heal. I still need time. Time will help, I know." She pulls herself together. The trembling quiets. "You may even have to repeat this year in school. But there's no excuse for violence. None. None!"

"It's only a three-day suspension. I'm going to do some reading in the library, and I'll use the time well, I swear. And I'll try to go to school afterward and do better."

She nods. "Dave, you're killing your chances for a good college, maybe for any college. You're killing your own dream, his dream, my dream."

"Don't worry, Mom. I'm in control, I promise. I'm not going to have to repeat this year. I'll use these three days really to learn something about Tennessee Williams."

She's glad that I'm interested in something. "And then?"

"I'll give school an honest try."

She takes my head in her hands and examines my face. "Did he hurt you?"

"He loosened a tooth." I wiggle it and show her. "But it feels better already."

"Tomorrow you go to the dentist and get it checked out."

"Mom—"

"I don't want a gap-toothed son." She manages a smile, then she's serious. "Dave, I believe in you. I wish I could be a better mother."

"You're doing fine," I say, and I clasp the hands holding my face. "Don't worry about it. You're doing just fine." What I truly mean is I know you are doing the best you can, Mom. And I am, too.

Both of us are whistling in the dark. For this one moment we do it together, and it helps.

I lose two hours of the first day of my suspension. Dr. Pearl keeps me waiting till I've read every issue of *People* in the rack and three issues of *Natural History*. Then it takes him all of about two minutes to determine that my tooth will survive. "Don't lead with your bicuspids," he advises me, and collapses at his own wit. Well, what do you expect from a guy who goes to college and then *chooses* to spend his life looking inside people's mouths? Imagination?

I buy myself a pack of 3 × 5 index cards. Carry them into a library and even if you are only in high school adults begin to take you seriously. I head for the public library. By the time I get there it is well into the afternoon. I run into Miss McKuen, head librarian, who is on duty at the reference desk. I couldn't have arranged it any better.

You've got to understand Miss McKuen. She is Cloverdale's number one character. Four generations of McKuens have lived here, something of a record because this is a town most people just pass through. Miss McKuen is a living reference book about the area. About anything. Ask her a question and she knows or she knows where to go to find the answer. Quicker than a computer.

She's an older lady, short and heavy but fast in her movements. She anticipates; she'd make a

74

great soccer goalie. Her short hair is gray and she wears the thickest glasses I ever saw. Her eyes are deep-set in wrinkles that she covers with really heavy make-up. She must love jewelry because she never wears less than three necklaces, big beads and stones and metal twists.

What Miss McKuen is most famous for is her traveling. Twice each year she takes a month and does some wild thing. Last year's trips were a safari to Kenya and white-water canoeing in Colorado. This year she took herself to the Galapagos Islands, where the bulb first blinked on in Charley Darwin's head. Giant tortoises live there and an incredible variety of finches: small songbirds like the sparrow. I guess you can learn something from anything. Imagine. He's looking at these finches. He sees that there are finches with a few different characteristics. He figures out that the differences are due to the peculiarities of the birds' separate habitats. The ones that survive are the ones that adapt. From this he guesses that the finches all come from a common ancestor. And he goes on to formulate the idea of *natural selection*. Elementary, my dear Watson.

How do I know all this? Miss McKuen likes to corner a person and tell about things. And she shows slides, in church, at home, in the library, anywhere there's a socket. Mom made me go the first time. That was after the Kenya safari, and there were incredible shots of elephant herds, lions, monkeys, and giraffes. Not one picture of Miss McKuen; she stays out of them. I'd go to a slide show of hers any time.

She is standing behind the checkout desk, hands in the huge, deep patch pockets of her blue corduroy jumper. She peers up at me. "David.

75

How nice to see you," she says. "How's your mother?"

"Fine, fine," I say, a bit confused because Mom must have been in earlier. She does morning hours in the children's room. Maybe Miss McKuen is working late shift and missed her.

"How can I help you?"

"I'm interested in the book *Remember Me to Tom.*"

She knows it at once. "An interesting but bad book. You'll find it under Williams in biography." She nods to her left.

"And maybe other biographies of writers," I say.

"Well, there are always the encyclopedias for short sketches. Then there are the book-length biographies." She nods left again. "And finally there are literary histories and that kind of thing if you look around 810 through 812. Just peruse the shelves till you find what you want. Or use the card catalogue. Our collection is not enormous but you'll probably find what you're looking for."

"Thanks, Miss McKuen."

"David, how come you're here during school hours?"

"I'm doing a special project," I mumble. "I have three days off for it."

"That's unusual. Mother know about it?"

I nod and move on.

I spend those next days in the twilight zone. First I read the Williams book and I am swamped by it. Sandbagged. What a life! His father hates him. He calls him "Miss Nancy" because the kid prefers reading and writing to sports. He breaks up his son's long friendship with a girl. For nothing! When the doctors do the lobotomy on the writer's sister, Rose, who is mentally ill, my eyes blur. I can't read it. I don't make a single note on my index cards because I'll remember it all, always.

When I'm finished with Williams I begin to look up some others, and I take a few notes about each.

Charles Dickens: His father was imprisoned for debts. The whole family lived in Marshalsea Prison, and Dickens, at twelve, was allowed to go out to work in a blacking factory, labelling bottles.

Edgar Allan Poe: His father disappeared right after he was born, abandoning his mother and her three children. He was adopted by John Allan, a man he grew to hate.

John Keats: His father, who operated a livery stable, died from a riding accident when John was nine. John himself died at twenty-six of consumption.

Herman Melville: His father died when he was thirteen.

Nathaniel Hawthorne: His father, a sea captain, died when he was four.

Lord Byron: His father died when he was three.

Jack London: His father denied his fatherhood and wouldn't marry Jack's mother.

Robert Louis Stevenson had dreadful violent fights with his father.

Franz Kafka hated his father and wrote about it all his life!

Enough! I stop looking up people. In fact, I tear up the index cards, but the notes are indelible in my mind. A wacky thought comes to me, and I laugh out loud in the silent library. A bent old guy reading *The Wall Street Journal* through a big magnifying glass gives me a dirty look. But it is funny; it occurs to me that I can probably be a great writer.

I've already got the family qualifications. Trouble, that's what does it. And we got trouble. Riley is right. I am just now noticing what was around me all my life; trouble had to hit me directly for me to notice. I had it too good so I grew up selfish. In that way, too, I'm like the Big Man.

I leave the library early and start for home thinking about Mom. Something has to be done about her. Here it is March already, blowy, wet, and bone-chilling. Curran, Hogan, and Hamilton, attorneys in Nome, Alaska, have been sending her packets of papers to be signed and returned. The divorce is in the works and when it's over she gets a big consolation prize: me! Here it is three months after D (Desertion) Day and she is still in permanent retreat. I, at least, go walking with Riley or Bean, and sometimes I toss a basketball around with Bean. My mouth is healed, and I won't fight again. I'm about half with it. Well, about a third.

Not Mom. She's even given up getting dressed when she's around the house. Jeans and a floppy shirt and running shoes are what she wears. They're what I wear and there's nothing wrong with them. Except Mom wouldn't have worn them before as everyday clothes.

When I come in I hear her voice; she is on the phone cancelling our subscription to the *New York Times*. In the old days she couldn't wait till she got Dad and me off mornings so she could sit over coffee and read the paper front to back. Now she tells the *Times* person on the phone, "I haven't time for it." But Mom, time is all you do have, I think, but I keep my mouth shut. The *Burpee's Catalogue* came weeks ago and there it is still in its wrapper on the hall stand. Other years she'd grab it and go mad with plans for the garden: roses, sweet peas, mums, along with great vegetables. "How about rhubarb?" she'd ask. I detest rhubarb. "Okra?" Dad would groan because he hated slimy foods. Then she'd stop teasing and she'd plant vegetables that we all love: tomatoes, lettuce, beans, normal vegetables.

"What are you going to plant this year, Mom?" I ask her, after the catalogue has been lying there for a week or so.

"I'll see."

I give it a couple of days. Then, while I'm eating salad I tell her the truth. "Those cherry tomatoes from your garden last year sure beat these." I'm trying to be subtle.

"Thanks." She smiles at me vaguely as if we're both not there.

She shops for food, and she cooks, and cleans, and she talks to me, but nothing registers. When she's not doing chores, she just sits. She doesn't watch TV or listen to her favorite chamber music; she just sits in her bedroom with the shades drawn, thinking. And she smokes. No one comes to see her. Even those goony birds who pecked up all my vital statistics when they were here have disappeared. She didn't encourage them. We have no family nearby. Uncle Kurt and his five children live in Utah. Aunt Rosalie, my father's sister, lives in Boston, but Dad and she never got on, so we're not close. It seems to be up to me to take charge of my guardian.

I've held off as long as I could. I really don't want to butt in on anyone else's life, particularly my mother's. She's been so great about giving me space these last months I truly didn't want to crowd her. And I believe in homely old Thoreau's advice: "If a man does not keep pace with his companions, perhaps it is because he hears a different drummer. Let him step to the music which he hears . . ." Those are practically the only lines I remember from English class this year. (Of course, I haven't been there that much.) Poor old Henry. What a way to go down in history, a fine mind and an ugly face.

I decide to go back to the library after dinner and talk to Miss McKuen. Boy, will she be surprised to see me again so soon. But Mom has worked as volunteer for her for a long time and she knows Mom well. She values Mom not only because there is never enough money in the town budget for adequate staff, but because Mom loves books and kids.

Mom is fond of Miss McKuen and respects her immensely, though my father's judgment was that the head librarian "is an opinionated old maid." He's right, but so what? She's interesting and she helps people learn about things. And she's fun in a bizarre way.

I come into the library quietly. It is deserted. She is sitting at the reference desk reading, of all things, *Frankenstein,* holding it about two inches from her face, really grabbed by it. She never hears me.

"Miss McKuen?"

Up she goes about a foot in the air, in terror. "I didn't hear you come in," she says. "I'm surprised—and, of course, delighted to see you so soon."

I make a fatal mistake. "That must be a good book."

She gives me a big smile and puts a marker in the book and shuts it. Probably she thinks I have an hour to spare to hear about Frankenstein. I'm sorry to disappoint her. A bright blue fingernail points to the book's title. I look closer. All her fingernails are shiny blue.

"Just renewing a friendship with the first thriller I ever read," she says. "Mary Wollstonecraft Shelley was nineteen years old when she wrote this book. It was kind of a bet."

Already, she's got me. "A bet?"

"Yes. She and her husband and the poet Byron were on a holiday in Switzerland in 1816 and it rained a lot. They were entertaining themselves by reading ghost stories. Then Byron suggested they each try to write a story. At first, she had no ideas. Every morning her husband would ask her if she'd thought up a story and she had to say no. Then the Frankenstein idea came to her in a dream."

"I saw the movie *Dracula,* Miss McKuen, but I never saw or read *Frankenstein.*"

"You'd be surprised at how different movies are from the books they come from," she says. "Here, borrow this. We can talk about it afterward."

"But you're right in the middle of it," I protest.

"The library owns two copies. And the other, the one I should be reading with my poor eyesight, is in large print. I just don't read it at the desk because of vanity."

Before I can get out of it she charges the book out to me and hands it over. That's what I really need. *Frankenstein!*

"How are you, David? How's your mother's health?"

Peculiar question. Second time today she's asking about someone who worked here this morning. Or did she?

"Okay," I say. Then I ask because it's the

only way to find out, "Isn't Mom working here mornings?"

Now she's surprised. "Not for some time now. She said she was feeling run-down and tired and she wanted some rest."

It's worse than I thought. Mom is keeping herself locked in day and night. And she doesn't tell me. We live like strangers in the same boarding house. "Not okay," I say to Miss McKuen. "Mom and I, we're very un-okay."

"I suspected as much. Come and sit." She points a blue nail at the chair beside the desk. "We won't be disturbed. Almost no one wants to learn anything obscure these days. You school kids aren't doing papers yet, and the adults have their computer tie-ins."

I sit. She waits. I stall.

"So?" she says, to prompt me.

I spit it all out in a rush. "My father's left my mother and me and taken off for Alaska."

Tapping a pencil on the desk, she eyes me steadily. "So that explains it. That's why she stopped volunteering here. When did this happen?"

"Before Christmas."

"But your mother worked right through the holiday. She did the story hours and the Christmas party. She baked batches of cookies. She was marvelous right through December."

"You know Mom. If she says she'll do something, she does it. No matter what."

"No matter what," she repeats softly with great sadness; "no matter what." Then she's her old crusty self again. "Tell me what's happening at home, frankly."

So I give out the whole sad story as I see it: the smoking, the sitting in the darkened room, the

82

loneliness, the untouched *Burpee's Catalogue,* the cancelled *Times,* and her saying she's reading—without books.

"I'm glad you've come, David. I wish you'd come sooner. I've phoned a number of times, but your mother is always polite and distant. And brusque. So I knew there was something radically wrong. That's not her character. But I didn't know it was *this.* I'll come by your house Thursday night. I'd come earlier but I'm on nights here. I'll be there after dinner Thursday. You be sure to be home."

"Shall I tell Mom?"

"Not a word." She grins mischievously. "She'd split."

Miss McKuen is a character.

I start to leave. I almost make it, but she pursues me down the steps.

I have forgotten *Frankenstein.*

Riley is in Rockabye, the jazz-rock ensemble. It's a community activity rather than a school activity because there's no money to pay a faculty advisor. The school lends the rehearsal space, and the janitor, and occasionally the dean, monitor the group. Two afternoons from three to six the members rehearse in the auditorium. Sometimes when I am in school, while Bean and the team are in basketball practice and I don't want to hear the shouts of the scrimmage or the thumping around in the gym, I sit in the back row and listen. The punk rockers are good and the Mick Jagger imitators are terrible. It's a mixed group and everyone is doing his own thing. Some of the kids are loudmouths, full of curses. Some are clowns. Most are dead serious about their music. A few are really out of it—on drugs.

But Riley? Riley's the best. She's a natural. Adriana, one of the punks—all pink hair—lends Riley her acoustic guitar and has taught her to play basic chords. Adriana looks like the worst, but it's weird how nice she is. Teachers give her a hard time; it's as if they can't understand that pink hair can be on top of a very nice person. Why does Adriana have pink hair? She says it's part of her karma, her destiny, her reward for what she did in her last life. I don't know about karma, but it is her own business. I mean—why do little old ladies including some teachers have white hair with bluing in it? It's their business.

Riley accompanies herself with simple chords and does great things with her voice. She's been writing songs like crazy, one of the few performers in Rockabye to sing original stuff. Of her songs that I've heard so far, "One More Renaissance" is my favorite. In fact, it gives me chills when she sings it.

ONE MORE RENAISSANCE

Don't it seem today
Like everything is running down?
The planet chokes in its own poisons
The gods have all gone underground
With the kids becoming square
And the rock becoming chic
And the smell of smug self-satisfaction reeks

Has each forgotten what he really wants again
And is this now the burning out
Before the very end?
Or will we get yet another chance
One more renaissance
Another renaissance
Just one more renaissance

Perhaps you've heard these tired words
Spoken by someone before
Well, they cut across the ages
Don't surprise much anymore
The same old worn-out ritual
Of reasoning and rhyme
But that slap across the face
Awakes us most every time
And perhaps it will seem new

For perhaps we are so young
We forget what has already been sung

Was there a time when many voices really rang?
And is this now the whimper before the final bang?
Have we started being dead in advance?
Or could there be one more renaissance?
Would like to see one more renaissance
Return to innocence
Our renaissance.

Riley dreams about owning a guitar but guitars
cost. The Rogers's budget couldn't do it even if Mrs.
Rogers said yes, and she never would. And Riley
wouldn't ask. She's saving for it, but babysitting
rates are low and high school expenses are high.

Then it comes to me, the second most brilliant
idea of the year! The first was telling Miss McKuen
about Mom; I just have this feeling that things have
to get better now. But this new idea, this brain-
storm, really knocks me silly. We have an unem-
ployed guitar in our attic!

I actually lure Mom into a real, lengthy conversation. After dinner I wait till she's sitting over a
cigarette and coffee. "Mom," I start, "I have a
terrific idea."

Slowly she returns from the shelter where her
mind hides. "Mmm?"

"You remember that old guitar up in the
attic?"

Her face gets that pinched look when she
remembers whose guitar it is. "Yes."

"Well, no one is ever going to use it here, and
Riley Rogers is singing in Rockabye at school and
she doesn't have a guitar."

"Can she play?"

"Some. She's learning. She's picked up a lot from other kids already."

Mom thinks about it for a while. "I don't see why you shouldn't give it to her. It's useless up there."

"Give?" I say. "I meant lend it to her."

It takes some effort for her to go on but she makes it. Just a single spasm of pain twists her face and then she's okay again. "No. You can give it to her. No one here is ever going to want it." She tries a joke. "Unless you plan on a singing career."

I sing so flat I stagger music teachers. Whenever it's do-re-mi testing time for choral work there's always a huddle at the piano as the examiner calls in colleagues. No one smiles. They listen in awe. A few cringe. That's one other way I am different from him. Two ways so far: I don't make casual friends easily, and I can't sing. Negative differences? Yes, but I'm beginning to value them because I think they tell me what's me.

"Go ahead and give it to her," Mom says. "It's a good idea."

We practically flew over that first hurdle. Now comes the high jump. "I was hoping we could give it to her together."

"We?" Mom is bewildered. "I know Bean very well, Dave, but I hardly know his sister. She's never been here to the house."

"It's kind of complicated."

"Everything seems to be," she says wearily, and gets up. I'm scared that's it, but she just fills her coffee cup again and sits back down.

"Well—Riley's mother has this thing about Rockabye, this phobia. She hates it and she hates Riley being in it."

I can see that Mom is actually staying the course; she's interested.

"Why?"

"Mrs. Rogers thinks popular music is noisy and obscene and evil."

"It's certainly noisy," Mom says. "You know I'm not crazy about it myself. But I don't think it's evil. I don't think it's dangerous."

"Mrs. Rogers is so set against it, I thought—"

"That if I were one of the donors, Mrs. Rogers might allow her daughter to accept?"

"You got it."

She shakes her head. I'm losing. "I don't know, Dave. I don't like to interfere in another family's affairs."

"How is it interfering if we give Riley a present?"

"It's interfering." She drifts off for a while and I think everything is lost; then she comes back. "How badly does she want—or need—a guitar?"

"Come pick me up after school tomorrow. Five-thirty. Look for me in the back of the auditorium. Hear for yourself."

At five-thirty on the digit, Mom appears. I see her before she sees me. She stands in the doorway lit by the exit sign. She's very pale but looking nice, head high, searching; she's dressed in a suit and high-heeled shoes, first time this year. She looks older; no more Sandra Dee. The set of her shoulders and the tenseness of her face make me scramble through the row fast to get to her. Once she sees me coming toward her in the dimness, she smiles and it's almost the old mom. I wish the smell of pot was not so powerful. I lead her to a seat in the back row. We sit through four punk numbers, bombing-raid decibels. Mom pays particular attention to Adriana, who is leader of the group and

88

who gives it all she has. "She's powerful," Mom says, "and disturbing."

Then it's Riley's turn. She comes up front with Adriana's acoustic guitar and sits on the edge of the platform, feet dangling: a long, thin, pretty girl with glossy black hair, a turned-up nose, and glowing blue eyes. She sings "One More Renaissance," then says she'd like to try a song she's just finished. She's experimenting with different forms. Even the big-mouths pretty much shut up and listen. Riley has class.

"Cleave Together, Cleave Apart," she says, and sings.

> You don't know what to do at this juncture
> You like to work smoothly, leave no trace or
>   puncture
> You'd like to leave me with a clean break
> You didn't count on tears or heartache
> Averted eye, a tugging heart
> Cleave together, cleave apart.
>
> Your fingers glide along the fissure
> You know just where to apply pressure
> Thought you'd found a diamond in the rough
> But I'm not so precious, and not so tough
> Reappraisal and restart
> Cleave together . . .
>
> You polished me into ice
> Now I'm cold at any price
> Do you want to sell it
> Or nestle it in velvet?
>
> A wry smile can split a heart in two
> The victory belongs to you
> Shards that glisten, each a crystal dart
> Cleave together, cleave apart.

After her turn, Mom and I slip out.

"Yes, she needs a guitar," Mom says. "The girl has a lovely voice and a sensitive, original style."

I almost grab her and hug her. But we are in public, in the schoolyard! Nobody is around, but if you hug your mother kids come out of all the corners. I squeeze her hand.

We go home and I bring the guitar down from the attic and we clean it up. It's a Fender guitar. I have no idea if it's good or junky but it doesn't matter. It beats not having one. The guitar is battered, but the wood glows and the instrument has style. I remember when I was a little kid he used to play it and we would sing "Clementine," and "The Blue Tail Fly," and "Puff, the Magic Dragon."

Why'd he have to run off and spoil our lives? If only someone could answer that question for me. And not with *Love; he fell in love.* Because that's no answer. Because if love hurts other people so badly, then that love is bad. Flowers growing in a cemetery are pretty but they are the flowers of death; they are not the same as wild flowers or lovely garden flowers.

About eight that night we take the guitar over to the Rogers's house. I have it all planned. I know Bean is doing research in the library, and Riley has a babysitting job with twins. (She gets paid double, but the kids are monsters. They communicate without talking; they plot by telepathy, Riley swears.) Mrs. Rogers comes to the door. She is surprised to see me. She is amazed to see Mom.

"Mrs. Rogers, this is my mother, Anna Schlegel Smith." Mom smiles as I say it. It's probably the first time she's heard it.

They smile at one another politely, the way ladies do.

"David, no one is at home," Mrs. Rogers says, "except me."

"That's okay. It's you we came to see, Mrs. Rogers."

"Come in, come in." We're in the front hall and she wants to show us into the living room.

Mom stops her. "Please, we're only staying a moment. Forgive us for coming in on you without warning. We've brought this gift for your daughter and we want your permission to leave it."

Mrs. Rogers is swamped. "For Riley?"

"Yes," Mom goes on. "This is an old family guitar." She pauses to gather strength. "It belonged to my ex-husband, who no longer has use for it. David and I would like your daughter to have it."

"Yeah," I say. "Mrs. Rogers, we sure would."

"But why Riley?"

"I heard her sing today, in school, at the Rockabye rehearsal," Mom says. "I came to pick up David and I stayed to listen for a while. A lot of the music is brain-damaging, but Riley's songs are lovely. Your daughter has great talent."

Mrs. Rogers just stands there, her hands dangling at her sides, silent. I have never seen her at a loss before. She is always in control.

"I'm no lover of current music," Mom says. "Classical music is *real* music to me. But your daughter's lyrics were moving—and original. She needs a guitar if she's going to do her songs justice."

Mrs. Rogers is breathing and functioning again. "I thank you for your thoughtfulness, particularly you, David, because I know this must be your idea."

I have nowhere to go, so I stand there and

suffer while the two ladies beam at me as if I've just discovered the cure for muscular dystrophy and retired Jerry Lewis from the tube.

Mrs. Rogers is uncertain. "I'm not sure Riley needs a guitar. She doesn't know how to play one."

"She does now," I say, "a little. She accompanies herself."

I see bewilderment in Mrs. Rogers's eyes. She told Riley she didn't want to hear anything about Rockabye. So she doesn't know. She cut herself out of it.

"Where did she learn to play?"

"From the others," I say. "They all teach each other."

"She's gifted," Mom says. "Please take this for her. David and I—we are so glad that it will be well-used."

Mrs. Rogers is still unsure. "Well, I certainly thank you on Riley's behalf." She stops, and I can tell she is trying to make up her mind which way to go. "I have serious doubts about Riley and this type of music. She sings in church, you know, and in the school chorus. We have always been very proud of her voice. It is God's great gift to her. I wouldn't like that gift abused."

Mom nods. "Your daughter's songs are strong and sweet. You need not be concerned. Perhaps you ought to hear them—as I did."

"No." Mrs. Rogers is determined. "I do not listen to popular music. As a matter of principle. But Riley may keep your guitar if she likes. She's old enough to make such decisions for herself. I won't prevent her from singing with that group. But I want no part of it."

Mom accepts that silently. We go.

"Thanks, Mom," I whisper outside.

"There's nothing we can do about it," she says. "It's too bad."

We're driving home in peaceful silence, me happy for Riley, imagining her face when she sees the guitar, Mom back in her cocoon (I think), when suddenly she says, "This is the first time since he left that I feel like my old self. Thank you, Dave." Her face is shining, wet.

Thank you, God, I say, over and over in my head.

Tonight Riley uses the Hot Line for the first time!

"Dave?"

"Yeah."

"It's Riley."

"I thought it was Cyndi Lauper."

"Very funny. I just want to say thanks for the guitar."

"You're welcome. We're glad to be rid of it."

"Ever think about the diplomatic corps for a career?" she asks me.

"Sorry. You're welcome, Riley. I—we—wanted you to have it."

"It means a lot to me."

"I know."

"I wanted to thank you in person but you were out of school."

"Yeah."

Long pause.

"I'd thank you more personally if you were near," she says.

"I'm not far." It's after midnight. I'm in my pajamas. "I could be near in ten minutes."

"It's late." She's scared now that she suggested it.

93

"Can you come down to your porch?"

"Yes," she says. "Come over. But don't trip on anything."

I slip my jeans on over my pajamas to save time, grab my sweat shirt, half-lace my running shoes, and I'm off.

She's already there, in her raincoat, long black hair loose, a lovely sight in the dim light. I've killed myself running and I can't even pant out loud.

"Thanks" is all she whispers, and I hold her to me and I kiss her like I've never kissed anyone, and I can't breathe and it doesn't matter because I just want to go on kissing her till I drop. Her mouth is soft and slightly Listeriney but I love it.

"I'll never forget what you and your mother did for me," she says softly, and she's crying. "I've got to go in now."

I kiss her again and then I watch her slip in and lock the door. She blows me a last kiss and is gone.

I am so glad I didn't go to school and get thanked there.

I go home—and I sleep.

Mom and I have dinner. She's made my favorite: fried chicken, french fries, cole slaw. Colonel Sanders's formula is talcum powder and sand compared to Mom's (learned from Grandma Smith). During dessert (Sara Lee chocolate cake—those Christmas sugar cookies were the last pastries baked in our house) Mom asks suddenly, "How was school today?"

"Okay. No sweat." How would I know? I stayed out today because I didn't get the homework assignments. I still cut pretty regularly. I won't flunk out. I just need to coast a bit. Till I get my head together. When you have a father for sixteen years and he scoots, you don't get him out of your head fast. No use my being in school when I can't fasten on what the teachers are saying. And I can't. My mind drifts about like a loose boat. As a result of all of this, what happened this afternoon was really the pits.

A big blowup between Bean and me. Lifetime friends and we argue all the time, but for fun; that's what friends are for. That's what makes us friends, the need to argue about everything and not get sore. This time it's serious.

I asked him to cover for me when I was cutting. It means if they pass the attendance list, as they occasionally do, he'd sign for me. He said, "No, I'm not covering for anyone anymore."

"But I'm not anyone. I'm your best friend."

"That's why," he says. "I'm not going to help you sit out your life. You want to do it, you do it on your own."

"Some friend you are."

"Better than you know." Off he goes, sore.

I think about it as I eat dinner. At first, I'm real mad. I'd do it for him.

I put him on the spot.

After I clear the table, I run upstairs and call him up. "Listen, Bean—" I jam up.

"The ears are Q-tipped and ready. Shoot."

"I'm sorry about today."

"No sweat."

"I put you on the spot."

"Forget it. Coming tomorrow?"

"I'll see."

"The great stall," he says. "Come to school, you cowardly twerp. Don't leave me to face Emily Dickinson alone!"

"See you."

"I hope so, Dave. Got to go."

" 'Bye." I go downstairs relieved.

Mom fools around in the kitchen till about seven-thirty. Then, what a surprise, she says, "I think I'll go upstairs and read."

No books have gone through that doorway in months; if she's reading up there it's the mattress label. Up she goes.

Shortly afterward, the front doorbell blares steadily as if it's being pressed by someone's leaning elbow. It stops and then starts again.

"David," Mom calls down, "please get that."

"Sure." I open the door and there is Miss

96

McKuen, as promised, with a pile of books in her arms that is awesome. She is just about to push the bell again with her elbow. For a second I am terrified that all the books are for me. I grab them as they're about to topple and I get a glimpse of an author's name: Maurice Sendak. I'm safe. He does children's books.

"Hi, Miss McKuen. It's nice to see you."

"Hello, David." She says it loud and clear. "I haven't seen you for a while. Mother home?"

"Yes, she's upstairs reading, Miss McKuen," I shout back at her, doing my best to bait Mom down.

It works. She starts to come down as I am taking Miss McKuen's fancy fur coat, white with fudge-colored balls scattered over it. I notice she's extra dressed up—five necklaces tonight. One looks like a string of blue marbles and exactly matches her nails.

"David, could you open a window?" she asks, screwing up her face to show disgust. "Someone has really befouled your nice living room with cigarette smoke."

Befouled? Methinks the lady doth jest. No one seriously talks that way.

"I hope you are not the smoker, David," she says severely.

"I'm afraid *I* am, Marcia," Mom says as she comes in.

"You?!" [*Attention Admissions Officer: I know I am not allowed to use two end punctuation marks in a sentence, but Miss McKuen's double take is the greatest. She could be a serious actress.*] "You?! But you don't smoke."

"I do these days. Please sit, Marcia. Dave, would you be a dear and set the kettle up for tea?"

97

Mom opens a bottom window and cold air rushes in, glorious, clean, cold winter air.

"I'd love a cup of tea—if you have herbal?" Miss McKuen tilts her head slightly, signalling me to move it.

I set up the stuff for their tea on a tray and I open a package of Pepperidge Farm Lidos and arrange them on a plate. I eat a couple of defective ones while I'm waiting, and before I know it seven are gone so I open a bag of Milanos and fill in the spaces. I don't taste the Milanos, not even the broken pieces. I can't believe I ate seven Lidos. Maybe Pepperidge Farm is shortweighting. I guess I did eat seven. The trouble is they're so small and my appetite is so big. If they were eclairs or napoleons, I'd never have eaten seven. While all this is going on I am straining to hear the conversation next door, but all I get are murmurs, and then the teapot whistles like a fire truck coming through the kitchen. Ready.

When I get back inside, Miss McKuen is into something big.

"I understand a lot more than you imagine, Ann—Anna—how could you allow your name to be amputated? Anna is a lovely name. Lemon Soother tea, I smell it. Let it steep. It's delightful tea. So, remember, I am sixty-two years old. When I was a girl I had dreams, lovely romantic dreams. Not mine originally. Society's. So they became mine. But life did not give me a husband and children though I wanted them awfully. In my generation that meant failure. The men who were interested in me were duds. The ones I liked always thought me odd. At thirty-one I became engaged to Arthur, a widower, an economics professor who was pleasant, kind, and the most boring man in the

98

world. He talked to me in outlines: 'A. The day is cold; A, sub 1. It might snow; A, sub 2. The snow will probably freeze.' And he would call out items for me to remember for him as if I were a memo pad: 'Marcia, remind me to buy paper clips. Make a note of that lecture time. Remember I have to call the periodontist.' I saw him as probably my last chance.'' She takes the tea Mom has just poured for her. ''I couldn't do that to him or myself. So I broke it off. He married soon afterward, a real estate agent, and they seem quite happy. I ran into them years later in Bloomingdale's and she was actually carrying a notepad and pencil in her hand. She was more amanuensis than wife in my eyes.'' Miss McKuen shudders dramatically. She measures one sugar then stirs and sips.

''Thank you for fixing the tray so nicely, Dave,'' Mom says. ''You're excused.''

''Nonsense. Get yourself a cup and come and join us, David. You're old enough to hear the lurid facts of my life,'' Miss McKuen says authoritatively. I hesitate. Mom's eyes show she doesn't mind. ''I order you to take a cookie or two and then go and get a mug for tea,'' Miss McKuen insists, and then she picks up one of each kind of cookie and forces them on me. I eat them though I've actually had enough Lidos. Then I do as she says.

When I'm all tea'd off (her joke), she picks up her story again. That's another thing about Miss McKuen. If she starts a story and there's an interruption, she just waits and continues it no matter how much later it is: weeks, months, I'll bet years. I can see her after an earthquake or some other disaster climbing up out of the rubble, saying, ''As I was telling you before this untoward interruption. . .'' and she's off again.

There is talk about retiring her but nobody should even think of that. She may be the sharpest mind we have in town. It is a New Jersey town, but even so.

"Once my Arthurian romance was over I realized that my medieval dreams needed renovating. The old ones wouldn't hold. It took me a while but I told myself, 'Marcia, since you don't share the Hindu belief in reincarnation this is your one time around. You can just mope it away longing for what can't be, or, since you are independent, you can live it as you please.'" She pauses to sip her tea and nibble a biscuit; I mean nibble. When women eat they take such small bites. Older women, I mean. Riley can eat a slice of pizza in four bites like me, but I bet once she gets older her mouth will shrink and she'll be chewing crumbs like Miss McKuen and Mom. How can you really get the taste of something in such small amounts? The feminists are wrong; there are certain very basic differences between men and women.

Miss McKuen eyes us fiercely. "Independence! That's the key word. The most important thing I ever learned and I pass it along to you. Try to be independent of purse and mind; the second is very hard without the first. Then you can *live* as you please. Don't hurt anyone and help wherever you can. Have a good time." She sips her tea for a while and then she's off onto other subjects, town trivia: the new cat-leashing ordinance and whether we need a bar in town when we already have four "package" stores. Chez Smith has not had such a lively evening since its pillar and main support took off for the land where they build ice houses without pillars or main supports.

Miss McKuen remains till eleven-thirty. She

gets herself invited to dinner next week, same time, after she gets off from work.

"I think I'll try a foreign dinner," Mom says slowly. "Maybe French. David is taking French. In his honor. I've always wanted to do it."

"We have the best French cookbook in the world in our library. *Larousse Gastronomique.* Come by tomorrow and pick it up," Miss McKuen says. "I'll bring the dessert," she decides.

I'm staggered by this French idea. If she always wanted to try it, why didn't she? Who stopped her? No one. Maybe Dad and I wouldn't have been enthusiastic about peculiar new dishes, but nobody actually stopped her. She didn't do it because she always wanted to please. Us.

Miss McKuen just sort of scoops Mom up out of hopelessness and carries her along. "Why doesn't David invite a friend?" she suggests. "Just so he won't be outnumbered by the smarter sex."

Two guests is practically a party. I figure Mom will say no. Parties are difficult in a morgue.

She surprises me. "Yes," she says, "that will be delightful."

"I'll ask Bean if he can come," I decide, but I doubt that he'll accept. He's a pizza-hamburger man like me.

"Bean?" Miss McKuen's right eyebrow becomes a question mark.

"Robert Rogers," I explain. "Bean because he sprouts so fast."

"Of course. You're sprouting pretty fast yourself, David. Soon you'll be taller than your dad."

First actual pronouncement of the name of the Departed in this room in my presence by a visitor. I do not respond.

She turns to the books she lugged in, a bunch

of newly-published children's books she wants Mom to review and estimate age levels for. "Many times," she says, "publishers' estimates of who can read what are way off."

Mom handles the books one by one absently. "I'd like to do it, Marcia, but I lack energy. I don't know when I'd get to them. These days any effort seems too much for me."

"There's no hurry. There's no long line waiting for books, you know. A nifty little invention called TV is giving us competition. But we're fighting back."

I take the fur coat out of the closet. I wonder as I handle it. Soft, warm, and expensive, but surprising. Miss McKuen is a conservation type; that's something else she shares with Mom. Isn't she against killing wild animals?

As she fits her arms into the sleeves, she looks at me shrewdly. "Fake fur," she says, "warm, hardy, and no living animal died so I could have it. It's a little *outré*, I know, but I don't want anyone seeing my coat to think it's real."

"It's nice," I say. "The design looks like Carvel Brown Bonnets."

She loves that. Even Mom is laughing. I don't see why it's so funny, but these days I take my laughs wherever and whenever I can get them. "Don't just laugh," I say. "Throw gold."

"I am so glad you came, Marcia." Mom sees her to the door.

"Me, too. Thanks for the tea. Now that I've found you out, you'll never get rid of me. I might even bring some slides over one night," she teases, looking sly. She knows her reputation. Fastest carousel in town—on her projector.

"I'd like that. Any time," I say.

"You have a gallant son, Anna." With that, she goes.

Gallant! Me!

As we're locking up Mom clicks into my everyday world for a second. "David, it's so late. Don't you have homework?"

"Nope." It's the truth. How would I know what the assignments are?

One thing I realize as I am getting ready for bed. All the time Miss McKuen was here, Mom did not smoke.

When I was a kid I used to imagine a guardian angel; she looked a lot like Glinda the Good in *The Wizard of Oz*. As I grew up she got younger and sexier; her bosom grew. Shows you what a limited mind I had. That's not the way she looks at all. She's short and heavyish, she wears a lot of make-up and blue fingernails, and she runs the town library in Cloverdale, New Jersey.

Miss McKuen and Bean coincidentally meet each other on the way over, so he comes in carrying a stack of Carvel boxes tied together and a Channel Thirteen cloth shopping bag bulging with books.

"I always *buy* desserts," she announces at the door. "My motto is 'Never do it yourself when you can buy it better done.' The last time I did a dessert was in 1935 when I toasted marshmallows with my Girl Scout troop. I burned them to a crisp." She makes me laugh. She can do anything she puts her mind to; what she's saying is she isn't into desserts. She takes the bundles from Bean. "There are a dozen Brown Bonnets in these boxes," she says, "to match my coat. It's an ensemble. Thanks, young man," she tells him. Mom breaks up at the "ensemble" line.

Bean is wearing: shirt, tie, and corduroy jacket. Mr. Manners. I stare at him till he pokes me. "Cut it out. My mother made me," he mumbles, as if I'd take that for an excuse.

We store the coat in the hall closet and the ice cream in the freezer and then we sit down to our French dinner: *salade Niçoise* (potatoes and string-beans cut fancy with anchovies, olives, and capers all doused with oil and vinegar dressing); *boeuf bourguignon* (incredible beef with onions and carrots and red wine); *pommes frites* (actual French fries); *haricots verts au gratin* (green beans baked in a casserole with cheese). I can't believe this food: Mom and Miss McKuen work on helping us to pronounce the names of the dishes.

Once we've got the names down, Bean and I provide very little conversation at dinner. We are stuffing ourselves. If the end of the world should come before dinner is finished, we don't want to have missed anything. I begin to formulate a theory about French culture and how it is the highest in Europe, undoubtedly. I mean—this food and the Napoleonic Code are *it*. I try to advance my theory but Bean is not having any of it. (He's taking Italian.) "This is all very delicious," he says, "but for overall culture you've got to give it to the Italians. I mean pizza, great soccer teams, and Michelangelo Buonarroti."

The argument ends right there because Michelangelo reminds Bean of a joke.

"You know," he starts, deadpan, "Pope Julius was looking for someone to paint the Sistine Chapel. So he sent for Michelangelo. 'Michelangelo Buonarroti,' he said, 'I have this great chapel. I want the painting in it to be the best, the most wonderful in the entire world. I want it to be so fine that people centuries from now will come to Rome, to St. Peter's, to admire the painting and to remember me, Pope Julius, a man of great vision and taste. I want it to be magnificent. So, Michelangelo Buonarroti, would you undertake to paint the Sistine Chapel for me?'

"And Michelangelo, without a moment's hesitation, answered, 'Sure tinga, Boss. Whatta color you want?' "

The ladies are in bad shape. They don't laugh at ethnic jokes. But it's so funny. So they break up and laugh, and since Bean is a guest he doesn't get called for it. I'm glad. Funny is funny and all groups have funny characteristics. Oh, I've heard many times how the jokes are hostile and put-downs. I suppose that's so, but I wish we could laugh at each other with pleasure. No harm meant. I sure don't think any less of Italians because of Bean's joke.

Suddenly I have an unexpected bad minute. "How's school?" Miss McKuen asks. "You boys beginning to think about choosing colleges?"

"Well," Bean says, "I have to be chosen. I need a basketball scholarship to be able to go."

"I'm thinking about it," I say fuzzily, and I stuff my mouth with *pommes frites,* making further speech impossible. Mom and Bean look uneasy. They both know something Miss McKuen doesn't. I'm an academic disaster this year. It's the unutterable truth.

We enjoy Miss McKuen's bought dessert. Bean and I eat Brown Bonnets galore.

The conversation ambles on. "I've reviewed those books you left and made a list," Mom says. "You were right, Marcia, about the age-grading. I think it's off in many instances. Of course, the publishers are gearing the books for national consumption. I think many of our local children are reading ahead of the national level."

Miss McKuen starts by saying how grateful she is. "I've brought you a new batch. It's in the Channel Thirteen bag. If you wouldn't mind looking them over . . ."

"I'd be glad to."

"I'm beginning to think about my next trip," Miss McKuen says. "I plan to take the summer off and go to India."

Mom gets up to refill the coffee cups. "India sounds wonderful. But not in the summer."

"It'll be hot. But I don't let weather affect me. I put it out of my mind. Otherwise, I wouldn't get to any of these places."

"Where will you go in India?" Mom asks, and I see the excitement in her eyes.

"Oh—Delhi, Agra, Calcutta, Benares, Bombay." She reels them off. "The great cities."

"Sarnath?" Mom asks. "Where the Buddha first preached?"

"Of course. And then there's a guru in southern India I'd like to have a look at. His followers believe he is God incarnate."

"Really?" Bean says. "God, Himself?"

"Yes, many millions follow him in India alone and there are others all over the world. He is reported to read minds, materialize objects, and raise the dead."

"I've always wanted to see India," Mom says slowly.

"Hey—want to come along?" Miss McKuen says. Just like that.

I told you: Glinda the Good. Right here in Cloverdale. Disguised as a librarian.

"Wow. India!" Bean is impressed. I'm pretty impressed, too.

Mom is very unsure. She looks at me. Up till

now I've always held with Dad's opinion that there is plenty to see right here in the good old USA. And there is: the national parks and the Great Lakes and Niagara and stuff. Last summer she wanted to go to Mexico and we talked her out of it. We watched the Yankees and we went to the Poconos instead. There is a lot to see here.

"I've dreamed about seeing the Taj Mahal," Mom says softly.

"Yeah, Mom," I say. "Go for it."

"Who told you about this guru, Miss McKuen?" Bean is intrigued.

"I came across some of his writings. I'm not a believer, but I am curious. Look, we hear so much about these tinsel types: Priscilla Presley and Madonna and Clint Eastwood. Inconsequentials. Who cares about them? Here is a spiritual leader who preaches universal love and equality, and says that each of us has a divine spark. I find the idea appealing. So I put belief on hold; the fascination gets me moving."

"Do you believe he can work miracles?" Bean wants to know.

"Hold that question till I—we—come back."

"We," Mom says quietly. "We. I'd love to go if we can arrange for David to have a fruitful summer."

"Don't worry about me, Mom. Go for it."

Miss McKuen is delighted.

"You have to be careful," I remind them. "It might be a cult like the Moonies."

"That's sweet of you, David." Miss McKuen is amused. "You think your mother and I might get sucked in, that we are looking for easy answers, explanations, systems."

"Isn't everyone?"

108

"No. Some of us learn to accept the limits of our understanding. I'm grateful for the world we have with its imperfections. But I am a busybody. I want to see for myself this holy man who exudes ash from his fingertips and makes gold rings materialize."

"Come to dinner next week," Mom says. "I'll try making a curry. And, maybe, a biryani. To acclimate us. Bean, you come, too."

Bean, who ate more tonight than three Parisians, works it out in his head. "I'd love to, Mrs. Smith, but I've got a game."

"I'll bring the hors d'oeuvres," Miss McKuen decides. "There's an Indian woman in Northvale who makes the most wonderful samosas: pastries filled with spicy vegetables."

"Wait a minute," I say. "What if I don't like this stuff? I've never even *tasted* Indian food."

"You'll love it, Dave," Mom assures me.

I have my doubts. This French dinner was pretty far out—and it turned out okay—for our house where the diet has always been out of Oak Park, Illinois. I eat tons of junk food but it, too, is basic American. Unless you count tortilla chips. Since the two women are so wild for the Indian stuff, I let it ride. There's always something in the refrigerator or in a can.

"Dave," Mom says, "how can I leave you alone here? How will you spend the summer?"

"I'm no mind reader like this Indian you're going to see, but I predict that I'll be going to summer school. To make up for certain small problems this semester. So, I'll guard the old homestead."

"You'll stay here by yourself?" Mom asks.

"Sure. I'm sixteen. Man of the house."

She's not enthusiastic but I'll work on her.

Time flashes by with Bean and Miss McKuen around. They set each other off. The evening is a pleasure. Out of consideration for our guests, Mom doesn't smoke. Mostly Bean and I listen to the two women rambling on about the library, the nation, the world. There is nothing Miss McKuen is not interested in and she takes you right along with her.

It's only when she and Bean are at the door, coats on and he with her bag of returned books in hand, that she nails me. "Read *Frankenstein* yet?"

"I've looked it over," I begin to mumble, "but I haven't had time to really get into it."

"We'll talk about it next week then. I'll look forward to that."

"Mmmmm." This is a commitment I am not looking forward to.

"All right, young men," she says, "I know how fond you are of trivia. What error did that book bring into the English language?"

Both women are smiling; they know the answer. I look at Bean and he looks at me. We lose. "Okay, okay," I say, "what error?"

"People think the monster's name is Frankenstein, but that's not so. That's the name of the scientist. His creator."

I like that. "His monster gets named for him and not even a 'Junior' like me."

"There's a word for that kind of naming," Bean says. I'm proud of him but, unfortunately, he can't remember it.

"Eponymous?" Mom suggests.

"Sounds more like a heavy African animal, Mom."

"Eponymous, from the word 'eponym'; it

means giving your name to a place or a thing," Mom persists.

How does she know that?

"Crossword puzzles," she says. "Eponym is a favorite six-letter word."

"Enjoy the book," Miss McKuen tells me. "Read it in a well-lit room."

Bean laughs a spooky monster laugh and they go.

"I think the idea of you two taking a trip to India is just great," I say, "and I'll be fine, here, by myself."

"Nice evening, Dave, altogether. Bean is sweet and Marcia is remarkable."

I agree. "You know, lady, you're no slouch yourself. That was an incredible dinner. And then you knew *eponymous*!"

Mom smiles. For a second it's like old times.

The unusual French food and the pleasant evening with friends leave me more hopeful than I've been. Yes, there is life after your parents' divorce.

But daylight dissipates the hope. I, who have not been able to concentrate on any required subject matter—not a book, not a magazine, not a class lecture—since the gent who taught me my ABC's has been eating his alphabet soup elsewhere, now have this screwy commitment. I have to read *Frankenstein* so Miss McKuen and I can discuss it. If it weren't Miss McKuen, who is the anchor keeping Mom from drifting off, I wouldn't give old Eponymous Frank a second thought. But I'm trapped.

I try working up plausible excuses. I'm busy with schoolwork. I don't care for Mary Shelley's writing style—too romantic. Gothics aren't my thing.

I dump the problem on Riley while we're finishing a mushroom-and-pepperoni pizza in the Edison Pizzeria. The tables are filled with kids from the high school, poking, squealing, smoking, giggling. Riley could sit at other tables; the Rockabye kids are there and some others she knows. She comes in with me and sits with me. No one asks to join us. I give off evil rays: Stay away. Smith smites!

"Riley, how am I going to get out of this thing?"

"Don't even try. Read the book. There's nothing to it."

"Books put me to sleep these days."

"Not this book. This one will keep you up."

"Not me."

"I saw this old movie on TV. With Boris Karloff." Her eyes widen as she recreates the monster's lines. " 'Oh Frankenstein. Remember that I am thy creature . . . I was benevolent and good; misery made me a fiend. Make me happy and I shall again be virtuous.'

" 'Be gone. I will not hear you. There can be no community between you and me. We are enemies.' "

"Sounds heavy," I admit.

"I read the book afterward. It's much better than the movie."

"Why don't you tell me about it?" I work at separating a slice from the pie.

Riley gives me a frown that's high on the Richter scale. She waits a while before she answers; then she lets me have it. "I shouldn't even bother to answer that but I will. First, if I tell you about it it will spoil the book for you forever; second, Miss McKuen will know the minute you open your mouth that you didn't read it; third, it's dishonest. If you want to be dishonest be smart about it. Go read *Masterplots.*"

That's the ultimate put-down. Riley, Bean, and I look down on the kids who use Barron's outlines, and *Masterplots,* and other cribs. We respect our brains enough to stay away from baby versions of grown-up material.

"*Masterplots* is in the library; she'll see me," I say, embarrassed. "All right, all right already, I was only kidding."

She chews her pizza crust and looks at me speculatively. "Maybe you were and maybe you weren't. You're changing, Dave. You're letting what happened turn you into a wimp."

"Thank you for those kind words of encouragement."

She grins. "I'm looking forward to hearing your book report."

"Uh-uh. You don't tell me. I don't tell you."

She shrugs. "That's okay. I already know."

I have to give the book a try. It's hard going. I sit in my room at my desk because the upholstered armchair is too much like a bed. Sixty watts are in the gooseneck lamp blazing over me like a sun. I don't fall asleep. Mary Shelley gets points for that. The first pages need to be gone over and over. It's a slow beginning. Slow? It creeps infinitesimally. I read: the Arctic wastes. This English explorer, Walton, sees a dogsled with a big, weird driver way in the distance Then traffic gets heavy; another dogsled with a sick driver, Victor Frankenstein, comes along, and when he hears about the first sled he gets all excited. It's his monster out there. While he's staying with Walton, iced in and very ill, Frankenstein tells the story of how he, a scientist, created this creature and gave it life.

I sort of like the creature. I feel sorry for him. Frankenstein makes him, and then doesn't want him around, so he's lonely. The creature wants friends, love. When he's first created that's all he's looking for: ordinary human kindness. Then Frankenstein drives him away; he's persecuted everywhere, an outcast whom no one wants. Wherever he goes they chase him away. So he turns into a monster.

The middle section of the book goes quickly.

114

The monster asks Frankenstein to create him a wife so he won't be alone. Frankenstein does it, but then he's afraid of being responsible for a race of monsters so he destroys her.

The monster vows revenge. "Remember—I will be with you on your wedding night." And in despair he begins to commit murder and other terrible crimes.

I practically race through the rest of the book. It takes me three nights. I end up on the monster's side when he says that Frankenstein's crime is the greater crime because he created a man without love, or friend, or soul.

I find myself actually looking forward to Miss McKuen's visit.

The Indian dinner is living fire, delicious but very hot. I extinguish the inner blaze with about a gallon of water taken in frequent gulps. Afterward, Mom insists that Miss McKuen and I stay at table while she clears up.

To my very great pleasure, Miss McKuen agrees with me. The monster is much wronged. And she knows so much! "Byron and the Shelleys sat around a blazing wood fire, during their wet Swiss holiday, and they discussed all sorts of wonderful ideas. What is the nature of the principle of life? Will it ever be discovered? Will the power of giving life ever be acquired? Would it be possible to reanimate a corpse? Galvanism, a theory about applying electricity to the body, was popular then and it implied such possibilities to them."

"So what you're saying is this monster book is really a serious book, too?" I say. "I missed most of that."

"Well," she says, "it's an entertainment that has other levels. I see it really as a book about the scientist's power to alter nature. It's about the creator's responsibility for his creation."

She's right. I can see that. "I think then that it's also a book about what happens to an outcast—to a social reject," I say.

"Yes! You won't believe this because Shelley is now considered one of the greatest poets, but then he saw himself as society's reject. He had a hard time, and his wife mirrors some of that in the book."

"All that in a monster story," I say, returning the book to her. "Thanks, Miss McKuen. I enjoyed it." I really did. She is a good teacher. I tell her so. "The thing is you get excited about ideas. Very few teachers seem to. Mostly they're bored."

"So it has always been," she says. "I don't know why. Teachers dry up. Usually, there are a few good ones. A handful. You have to search them out."

The Regency, a movie house on upper Broadway in Manhattan, plays old movies, and one day I spot an advertisement for *The Bride of Frankenstein* with Boris Karloff and Elsa Lanchester. I take Riley on the bus into the city to see it. We buy the big size popcorn, which oddly is larger than the king size or the large size, and it's buttery and delicious. She hides her head in my shoulder whenever the movie gets scary. I love it. Afterward, I explain all the implications of the created monster to her and she is impressed. I don't quite give Miss McKuen full credit. I figure she doesn't need it—everyone knows she's a brain—but I do need it. And how.

Riley and I walk all the way up Broadway to the George Washington Bridge, holding hands, enjoying the city. We talk the entire time. A Spanish-speaking man offers to sell me a fresh red rose in a plastic tube for one dollar. "Pretty señorita," he says, and he smiles at Riley. I agree and I buy it. We have so much to say to each other we have to hold back and take turns and stop interrupting each other. Only once during that whole evening is there any strain. I ask her how things are going with Rockabye. Suddenly, she's a clam.

"It's okay," she says. "It's not what I thought it would be."

"How do you mean?"

"I'm not sure yet, Dave. I'm working it out in my head."

"Did something happen?"

"No. It's just different than I expected. My mother is a smarter lady than I gave her credit for."

A tall black kid goes by us on a skateboard and he's incredible, looping and jumping. We stop to watch. His feet are as fine-tuned as a ballet dancer's.

I figure I better drop the subject. When she's ready she'll open up.

This evening constitutes what is really my absolutely first, on-my-own, Mom-doesn't-drive date. Hers, too.

I'll never forget it.

The monster will always have a friend in me.

It's the middle of May, two weeks before the Decoration Day Rockabye concert. Riley phones me very late one night.

"Dave?"

"No. It's Cyndi Lauper."

"Listen—" She sounds very upset, as if she's been crying. "Would you think me a terrible wimp if I pulled out of the concert?"

I am amazed. "Yes. No. Why?"

"I can't do it. I just can't do this to my folks."

"You're not doing anything bad."

"You don't understand. They have their standards. And those are mostly my standards, too."

"What are we talking about, Riley?"

"Oh, about the fooling around and the cursing and the pot. Everything that goes on."

"But you don't do any of it. You don't even chew gum."

I don't get a laugh.

"I hear it and I smell it and I know it's happening. It becomes part of me. Mom thinks it damages me and lately I've been thinking she's right. It's not where I belong."

"Where do you belong, Riley?"

Long silence. "I don't know. Maybe singing gospel. Some girls in the church are forming a group."

"Why not after the concert? You only have two more weeks to go."

"Because everything is getting more intense and it's wrong for me. I've known it for a long time, but I was afraid to pull out. Yesterday I talked to Adriana. She's straight with me. She really likes my songs though they're weird for the group—and I am part of the program—but she says I should do what's right for me. I'm going to withdraw."

"Think about it for a day or two," I urge. "Don't decide in a hurry."

"I've been thinking about it for weeks. A concert where my mother won't come is not for me. Tonight Dad said he would come, but I know he'd hate it. The kids in the group are good musicians and some of their music is great, but it's just not worth it for me. The list of performers goes to the printer tomorrow. I don't want to be on it."

"You sure, Riley?"

"Sure."

"Just so you won't be sorry."

Long silence.

"They're good songs, Riley."

"I can sing them with the new group." Pause. "Dave, you want the guitar back?"

I get sore. "Hey, that's a gift from Mom and me. Go make heavenly music on it."

"You," she says, "are more than a friend."

"Riley," I warn her, "you are growing up to be like my mother. Too soft. Too vulnerable."

"Maybe that's why you like me," she suggests.

I sleep on that one.

My junior year ends just right for the hollow man— not with a bang but a whimper. I manage to get through English because Mrs. Aronson is a sucker for Tennessee Williams and for good writing. I do a last-minute critical essay, fueled by pure adrenaline, on three of his plays and it wows her. *"Where were you all term when we needed you?"* she writes on the last page at the end of her critique. "B," she writes; blessed B: divine curves on a vertical.

Away, Mrs. Aronson, I answer her in my head. Away. My mind fell in love with long distances. Forgive me.

I pass French because languages come easy to me and I cram for the final like a spy who's going to be grilled. Madame Simone is kind but firm. A good final; too many absences: one divine curve and no vertical. C. I am grateful. I do not look a given C horse in the mouth.

I fail calculus and modern European history. Calculus is, of course, inevitable. I had thought I could bluff my way through the history course, but my ignorance is awesome. I do not even attempt the final essay on the economic causes of World War I. I fail with style. No divine curves: one vertical and two small horizontals: F.

Dean Packard sends for me. He is not unkind but he puts it right to me. "You're killing yourself, Smith," he says. He's got my transcript on that neat desk. "Two and a half years ago you entered this school as college-track material. It's true you've only been here in patches because your folks move around, but you managed to keep your grades way up at first. There are even several notes in the file from schools you were a transient in saying you were good stuff. That's then. These days you're absent all the time, and when you aren't absent you aren't doing the work. Care to comment on any of this?"

"No, sir."

He shakes his head. "With your capacity it must have taken real effort to fail two majors."

I am silent.

"I want to see your mother." He remembers.

There's no way out. Mom goes and she comes home destroyed. Packard is polite but he doesn't spare her. She gets the word: Little David is an academic disaster. He wants her to do something radical before I self-destruct. Those are his words; she quotes them to me.

Mom feels terrible. "I should have been after you, Dave. I should have made you go to school. I should have seen to tutoring."

"You couldn't. Nobody could." I am telling her the truth. "I just wasn't with it this year. It's not a big tragedy. I'll take the two courses while you're away. It'll keep me busy."

"There's no use registering for summer courses unless you're going to go—and do the work. What we've done to your high school career is criminal. Criminal!" She can't forgive herself.

"I did it, Mom. *I* did it to myself."

"With a little help—from some relatives," she says sadly. "*Some* relatives."

"I'll do the work. I promise I'll do the work. I'll ace those two courses while you're gone."

"Two courses. Two! How can I go off and leave you in this situation? I should stay home where I belong. I wouldn't mind—"

She would do it, too. In one second she reverts to the lady who shrank her given name, ate all-American, and gave up all her rights to her charmer of a husband. Habits don't die; they lie in wait to trap us.

121

"—but I have a commitment to Marcia." She's tremendously upset.

"I know how much you want to go. If you don't go to India, then I don't go to summer school. We both stay home and fester. It means I don't go back next year because I am *not* going back as a junior. So I'll quit."

"Dave—"

"I mean it, Mom. I don't need you breathing down my neck all summer." What I mean is I don't want you to give up what you want to do just because you think I have a prior claim. Sometimes what a person needs for herself—even if she is a *mother*—is the prior claim. I can't talk about it anymore, but Miss McKuen puts it strong and loud.

"David does not need you," she says. "You promised to come abroad with me and we've made all our arrangements. I am holding you to your promise."

Mom is distraught. The mother-wife syndrome has paralyzed her.

"I want to be by myself," I tell her. "I'll do the work, I promise. In September I'll be a senior." I keep up the propaganda. At first she doesn't believe the summer school bit—really believe it—but I mean my promises and I convince her. At the time, I tell myself I'll do it for her because it is important to her. Not to me. To her. That's reason enough.

I make an insane silent resolution. I will not cut a single day of summer school. That is six weeks of classes five days a week. Penance for all those winter days I went walking on the flats.

Mom and Miss McKuen get all sorts of weird shots and pills and we spend a few crazy days getting the two of them organized—Mom cooks

and freezes all kinds of food for me just in case—
and then finally, finally they take off for India.

Last sight I have of Miss McKuen, she is wav-
ing a white chiffon scarf at me. I clasp my hands
above my head in a victory sign. I know a sad
secret. Last night Mom told it to me in absolute
confidence. Miss McKuen's eyesight is deteriorat-
ing. Her doctor gave her permission for this trip—
but it's to be her last biggie. No one else knows.
She felt she owed it to Mom to tell her, and Mom
decided that I had better know, too. "When we
come back, she's going to study Braille," Mom
said. "Just in case. She says she always wanted
to."

"How can she be so brave?" I asked.

"Habit," Mom said. "She's worked on it her
whole life."

Last sight of Mom I have she is going through
security check, her head turned back to look at
me, her eyes worried. I give her the hundred-
million-dollar smile. I know who I look like but I
can't help it. So I begin to jump up and down like
an idiot and wave and yell, "Good-bye! Good-
bye!" Stay well, Miss McKuen, I am saying in my
head. Stay well! Have a wonderful time! See everything! I know that my yelling and jumping up is
creating a weird spectacle and I am glad. This idiot
behavior is my own style.

I spend the summer alone in the house.

Bean takes a job waiting tables at the Jersey
shore; Riley carries the guitar to upstate New York
to be music counselor at Camp Susquehanna. Several times, Mrs. Rogers calls up to invite me to
come over and join them for Sunday dinner—"The
house is so empty," she says—but I refuse, politely. I just don't feel up to it.

I have never been so alone.

I register for modern European history and calculus so that I can be real honest-to-God senior in September. I walk in the flatlands, green now, and hot and dusty. Crickets talk to me. Mosquitoes dive-bomb me. No Bean to argue with. No Riley to call up. They write to me. I answer but my letters are dumb, boring.

One afternoon after classes I go into McDonald's in Pine, near the school, and there behind the counter is Adriana in a short uniform. I see she is letting the pink go out of her hair, but she's got it combed all spiky and strange, in points like stalagmites. She is wearing weird eye make-up that makes her look like a silent film actress—dark, dark shadows. When I tell her my mother is away and I am alone for the summer she offers to come over and visit anytime. In fact, she would be glad to help me keep house; her aunt, with whom she lives, couldn't care less.

"Thanks, Adriana," I manage to say, "but I'm not into socializing. My parents got divorced and I'm brutalized."

"Join the club," she says. "You're lucky your mother had space for you. But you don't have to suffer alone. I'd be glad to keep you company." She puts her hand over mine on the counter.

I shake my head. "It's a nice offer but I'm not ready for it."

"Anytime. When you want me, just whistle. Quicker—call me up." She brings my burger and an orange drink. I pay and take it to a table far from the counter because I'm embarrassed.

I like Adriana. I'm sorry for her, too. She's a smart, nice kid who got zapped. I'm just not her

124

speed. She's not even her own speed, but she doesn't know it.

As I'm eating, she comes to stand by the table. "You're Riley's best friend, aren't you?" she asks.

My mouth is full. I nod.

"Lucky Riley," she says, and back she goes.

In the house, alone, I talk to myself. I carry on the old argument with my father. Why? Why? Why? At night I talk to the TV. I leave it on for company even when I'm not watching. Late at night I get up and search the darkened house for the cause of spooky sounds. I am practically a hermit.

It's scary to think that some people live like this all the time, cut off from everything human. Old Thoreau did it for more than two years at Walden Pond practicing self-reliance. He can have it. I choose human company any day.

I nearly destroy myself studying. No, not really studying. Getting myself to study. Telling myself that I have to turn off the TV, turn off the stereo, sit at the desk, and work. I gain eight pounds in three weeks from junk food and my own cooking—Lay's potato chips destroy me—so I begin serious running to lose the lard. I actually learn to make good salads, with mushrooms, croutons, bean sprouts, and I get talked into trying tofu—bean curd—by a cute Japanese demonstrator in the supermarket.

Letters and postal cards pour in from Mom. All enthusiastic. The Taj Mahal is gorgeous. India is incredible. She gets to see the wonder-working holy man from a distance and his fingers do seem to exude ash. The experience is remarkable and she is unable to explain it. Ditto Miss McKuen. Divinity or sleight of hand? They don't know. They are surrounded by hundreds of pilgrims who believe. Absolutely.

Miss McKuen is feeling fine and is more energetic than Mom some days.

Am I eating sensibly and going to bed at reasonable hours? I write her air letters filled with yeses. Does she think I would say no?

I learn tangents and variables and Bolsheviks and Mensheviks and somehow I pass the two courses. Not brilliantly, but I pass respectably. I know these are baby steps, but I *am* walking. Man is inherently an upright creature, but I have been crawling about on my knees for a long time.

The travelers return and Mom has been liberated. She has given up smoking. She would not smoke near Miss McKuen—or anyone else who didn't smoke—and it got to be too much trouble. I am incredibly proud of her. No matter the reason, she's unhooked.

She is glowing with energy. Miss McKuen has convinced her to work at the library part-time (not as a volunteer but as a real salaried assistant librarian) and go back to school, this time to Miss McKuen's alma mater, the Columbia University School of Library Science. She wrote to them from India, and it seems to be possible. Her baby steps are much bigger than mine, but the two of us do seem to be coming up off the floor at last. At Miss McKuen's urging, she has set herself a goal: to be independent of *his* money even though she can have it.

I go back to school and I don't cut classes, but to tell the truth I am treading water just to keep from sinking. If Edison Regional gave letters for moving in place I surely would earn a major "E" for those first months of the senior year. I do all that is expected of me but it seems absolutely without meaning.

The thing is: I get myself to do it. Oscar Obedience, that's me. I'm crowding Mal Harris for the white gym socks/attendance record. I buy new spiral notebooks and I swear I'll keep neat notes and not draw Playboy bunnies in the margins. Every time my mind takes off for the far north I haul it back. Bean and Riley try to help; Riley calls me up nights just to hang out on the phone. She and four other girls have formed their gospel group; the minister of her church welcomes them and she's excited about it. They don't only sing religious songs, and they *love* her songs, especially the ones she made up during the summer for the kids at camp. Her mother is pretty happy, too. Bean is just there and that's enough. They show me they like me by being glad to have me among the living. That's more than enough. That's a lot.

What will I do when I finish high school?

This becomes, increasingly, a question of major world interest.

Will there be a nuclear war?

Will apartheid end in South Africa?

What will David Smith, Jr., do after high school? (Perhaps in reverse order of importance.)

Bean tries to talk to me. I tell him I don't want to discuss it.

Mom tries to talk to me. I tell her I don't want to discuss it.

Riley knows better than to try.

Miss McKuen tries to talk to me. Uh-uh. Not even Miss McKuen.

Everyone around me in school is gearing up for the big leap into life.

I might pump gas for a while. Sell pizza. Burgers. Take a year or two off. Lots of kids take time off.

Truthfully, I can't imagine why. I've always been ahead for my age in most things and so proud of it—and *he* was so proud of me—I grew up in a hurry to do it all. Can I change or is it in my metabolism? In my genes?

"I'll *see*," I say. "I'm thinking about it. Don't worry."

And I am thinking about it. I know what my academic record means. I know where it can take me, and I don't want to go there. In the Garden of Eden before the Alaskan Ice Age I spent hours and hours talking with my parents, particularly with my father, about college. I was headed for the best, the top, because that was the only reason to go to a liberal arts college. Not to prepare for a job or a profession. Not for any technical training. To learn. To become an educated, thinking, aware person. Fit citizen of a democracy. Sounds cornball, but we used to be a cornball family, All-American, Oak Park, Illinois, macho and Philadelphia, Pennsylvania, Quaker. Where could I go now? Nowhere first-rate. Not even second-rate. And third-rate doesn't make sense when it comes to learning.

The problem is not only my record. Something has happened in my head. I'm not sure what I can handle anymore. Ideas used to grip me so that I could be as hyped by a good discussion as I was by a basketball game. I'd listen to speakers scoring points and I'd be very excited, taking it all in, listening and learning and storing it away the way a camel stores water for later use. I am unable to care now. I try. I really do try. I think of the lobotomy they did to Rose, Tennessee Williams's sister, and I feel as if I've had one done on me, too. Some of me has been severed.

I am taking all the steps but I am not dancing. The only good hours of this hard time are spent in the advanced biology course, which Bean and Riley are also taking. Often we do our homework together and we enjoy Mrs. Zygoda's peculiarities. (She was our general science teacher centuries ago.) Here is a bizarre woman who thinks biology is more beautiful than symphonic music or great art. "Greater than Michelangelo?" Bean asks her, and I know he's ready to tell the Sistine Chapel joke, but she looks him in the eye solemnly and says without missing a beat, "Infinitely greater, Robert. I am admiring *original* creation." The thing about her is whenever she offers information she does it as if she is presenting us with magnificent priceless diamonds and other gems and entrusting them to us. How can anyone say no to diamonds? It's really fun to listen to her go on and on. After a while, she persuades us of the beauty of her treasure.

Early on in the semester she begins to talk about research papers. I hear her but I remain my usual tuned-out self. Put it off, put it off, the static blocks action. Didn't I save myself at the last minute with a wallop of a paper for Aronson?

Mrs. Zygoda moves the broadcast volume up to high. She's starting to talk topics. She's got to approve each person's project idea and there's a deadline. Like tomorrow.

Bean approaches me with a proposition. "Listen, Dave, I have this idea. I figure you owe me because you started me off on my obsession."

I look at him. The man is bonkers. "Me? What are you talking about?"

"You started me wondering about this sex-drive business."

I get hysterical. "Come on, Bean. You are merely entering what Zygoda would call 'delayed puberty.' "

"Entering nothing. I've been there forever in my mind. But I'm talking about Heathcliff. Out of control? Possessed? That business. The way people behave when they're in love. Like druggies."

I am very uncomfortable because I remember those first raw conversations going over and over what my father had done. Just this morning I wrote "Return to sender" on the miserable monthly airmail letter and zipped it back to its progenitor who is also my progenitor. It's hard to move on when what you think is past continually rises up to nail you in place.

"So—you've turned into a sex maniac. Bean the Ripper. Bean the Beast!"

It takes us both a while to recover from that vision.

"No, I'm cool personally. But I've decided to study aspects of the peculiar mating habits of some living creatures for my bio paper."

"Bean," I say, "I fear for that rice bowl you call your mind. Zygoda will never stand for it."

"I've already told her. She was not over-enthusiastic."

I'm awed. "What did she say?"

He puckers up his mouth. "Robert, you may do this dubious project, focusing on a specific area, of course, but you must have a parent read and sign the final draft before you submit it."

"Censorship," I say. "She's afraid you'll do a porn paper."

"Not a chance. I told her humans just aren't that interesting."

I hooted. That's why I like Bean. He's got a novel view of the world. Like he's nuts.

Turns out he's serious. "Really. I've been doing some reading and looking around. There are so many fascinating topics that I thought maybe you'd like to work with me. We could do a joint paper."

I'm suspicious. Is he trying to be a crutch for his handicapped friend, Dave?

He goes on. "You're a better writer—you'll do more of the putting it together on paper, which I hate—and I have some very good ideas about where to dig for the stuff and what to go after."

"Why didn't you ask Riley?"

"Are you kidding? I'm her brother. She can't even talk to me about binary fission without blushing. Think about it, Dave. Studying Mother Nature might take your mind off your troubles. Remember, she beats Michelangelo. 'Original creation, Robert,' " he imitates Zygoda.

"Sure tinga, boss. Whatta color you want?"

"At least consider it. You have no topic. Tomorrow's the day."

"That's the craziest idea I ever heard. Here I

am—the damaged result of the peculiar mating habits of primates—and you want me to concentrate on *that? Now?*"

"Choose something interesting," he suggests helpfully. "Fish? Birds? Reptiles? Insects? You wouldn't believe the wild tricks nature plays. I've just begun to look into the stuff and I'm hooked."

"For example?"

"Well—" Bean the lecturer takes over. His blue eyes are glowing and he's as excited as he'd be reporting a Knicks game. I swear he is probably going to end up a teacher. He loves, he LOVES to give you the word. "I read this stuff about the bird of paradise."

"Not *the* bird of paradise!" I make an appropriate about-to-barf face. "Anything but the bird of paradise!" I never even heard of the bird of paradise. He steamrollers me.

"These birds live in parts of Australia and New Guinea. Probably all their ancestors were crummy-looking brown or gray. The female birds are still that way, not very attractive. Way back in time where they lived, there was lots of food and no danger. So, what happened to them over hundreds and hundreds of years?"

"They got fatter and fatter till they had to go to bird health clubs?" I guess.

He looks at me with disgust. "In this nice safe place the lady birds chose the most attractive males to mate with. Over the generations this kept happening and the males got a chance to develop more and more elegant, colorful plumage. Today a male bird of paradise is positively punk. He's got elaborate plumes all over: head, back, throat, wings, tail. They can be green, orange, black, blue, or yellow. The ruffs become erect during courtship.

He flirts with his feathers spread out and he moves so there's a gorgeous iridescence. He hangs upside down or takes a horizontal position and does all sorts of tricks to attract the female. These days the males are pretty snazzy. The females watch the show and hold off till they decide on which is the flashiest, fanciest male. Then they go for him. The winners get all the girls so generation after generation they get more gorgeous."

"I feel for the losers," I say. There's no stopping him.

"Darwin noted this and he says this way the females decide what traits will evolve in the males. Of course, if there were larger predatory enemies or strong males to challenge the show-offs they might get eaten, so all this gorgeousness can't work for every species. Sometimes physical characteristics have to be a compromise."

"End of lecture?" I ask.

"One sec—" Bean digs around in his pockets and comes up with one of his many scraps of paper. "Darwin sets this idea down in two parts. Sexual selection is 'the power to charm the females,' and 'the power to conquer other males in battle.' That theory is what I am going to research."

I have to agree the material is interesting. And working with Bean is an appealing idea. Also, I have no good alternative.

I let him talk me into a conference with Zygoda. She is certainly not thrilled. But she's one of those principled teachers who doesn't believe in saying no to a student's idea if it's not completely off the wall. "I much prefer topics like the one your sister's taking," she tells Bean. "She has agreed to look into 'Life in Pond Water.' " With more strength than either of us has any idea he can muster, we don't laugh. We look at her earnestly. (Pond water! I'm dying. Riley is a saint! Saint Riley; the world really tries her and she doesn't let it spoil her.)

Zygoda questions us thoroughly to be sure we're not putting her on. "Very well," she says at last. "As long as a parent reads and signs the paper, David, you have my permission to work on this project."

This paper is going to have as many signers as the Declaration of Independence.

Mom loves the idea because when I tell her about it I am laughing myself silly. She sees it's beginning to grab me the way things used to, before. It's interesting to watch her these days. I think she's starting to be relieved that Dad ended their relationship. She is an honest person and it was not an honest relationship at the end. It must have been very hard for her to pretend that everything was perfect. What a bind she was in, thinking she had to put the best face on everything, and hope, and pretend, and be optimistic while the home she protected was shaking around her. Because she knew. I'm convinced she knew and it hurt her as she sat around and waited till the walls came tumbling down.

"I'll sign the paper with pleasure," she says. "I know it's going to be original and wonderful. I can't wait to read it."

"Whoa. First we have to write it, lady."

"Hurry," she says.

That's my mom.

Bean and I do a lot of general background reading as we search around for appropriate material. Miss McKuen is better than the Smithsonian as a research resource; she knows where to find almost everything. I begin to dig in. Those weeks I am working on the biology paper are a happy time for me. *Escape,* Bean accuses me when I still refuse to talk about the future—and when I miss the deadline for filing for the next SAT exam—and he is right. Whoever said a good escape was a bad thing?

Bean is still intrigued with *sexual selection.* He is paging through *The Descent of Man,* and he gets all involved with examples like the male stickleback fish, a gutsy little fighter that Darwin says "has been described as 'mad with delight,' when the female comes out of her hiding-place and surveys the nest which he had made for her." Superstickleback fights off the other fish and gets the girl.

Bean picks up all kinds of exotic information and he's brimming with it. I never know what's coming, birds of paradise, flies, bees, salmon, sticklebacks.

Many topics interest me and that's a problem. I have to narrow my share to a size I can handle. Oddly enough, I read about ants and their swarming and that grabs me. Ants! I never gave ants a single thought. Why would I?

Turns out that there is one day a year in late spring or early summer in our part of the world when there is tremendous excitement in every ant colony. That means a few dozen to half a million ants. All the ants rush around but the most excited ones are the winged males and the females, the queens. They're dying to take off; their transparent wings vibrate. It's mating day!

No one knows what starts the swarming, but when it comes the crowds of winged males and females escape and fly up, rising in huge dark billows.

The males go first. The females, heavy with eggs, hang back. This stops inbreeding because by the time the females of a colony are aloft the males are gone. So the females mate with males of another colony.

Even the infertile females without wings are trying to fly: they run out and jump up and try to beat the wings they don't have. (I feel sorry for them.) After the flying males and females have mated, they drop to earth. The males crawl off to die, unneeded. The fertilized queen sets out to build her nest and raise offspring. She bites or scrapes off her wings and gets to work. She's now capable of laying eggs continuously all her life for as much as fifteen years.

It's kind of eerie how the males are not needed or wanted after reproduction.

I tell Miss McKuen that and she says, "Wait, you haven't seen anything yet," and she brings me an old, beat-up book by a French entomologist, Henri Fabre. "The best," she says, "the very best nature writing in the whole world."

Well, she's inclined to be overenthusiastic.

I begin to read and you know what? She is

right. From what I read, I get what Bean calls my "morbidly fascinating topic": *disposable males.*

Fabre is discussing the praying mantis, a kind of grasshopper. I take careful notes and I read them to Bean. His turn to listen. "The mantis is green and brown and it blends with the foilage. It just stands motionless and waits for its food: other insects. It stands with its front legs folded near its head, and those legs are spiky, razor sharp, and hooked. It looks like it's saying a prayer. After mating the female mantis turns her head around and bites the male in the neck and starts chewing."

"Yuck," Bean says.

"Yeah. She eats everything except the wings."

"Fussy eater," Bean says. "My mother wouldn't let her get away with it."

"This guy, Fabre, stayed on one female's case for two weeks," I tell him. "She mated with and finished off seven husbands."

He refuses to believe seven so I go get the book. It's pretty wild and Fabre's writing makes it wonderful. He doesn't write the way other text-book writers do. His best line is:

> She [the mantis] takes them all to her bosom and makes them all pay for the nuptial ecstasy with their lives.

"He's talking about a grasshopper," I say. "The man's a mad poet."

"You think the males know beforehand?" Bean wonders.

I shrug. "It doesn't matter. They can't help themselves. I'm going to stay with *disposable males.* I'll look into spiders and scorpions. Fabre has a great section on scorpions. And there must be more."

Bean goes mad with his theory. "Creatures mating under those conditions are possessed, just like that jealous Bishop of Aquila who turned Princess Isabeau into a falcon each sunrise and her lover, Navarre, into a black wolf each sunset. Remember *Ladyhawke*?"

"That was fantasy, imbecile. A story. Unreal."

"Reality is going to turn out to be wilder. Isn't this the best project anyone ever thought of, Dave? We'll drive Zygoda wild wondering. . . . Let's not tell her anything except the bare topics. Let her wonder."

I tell Riley I'm going to concentrate on disposable males.

"Remember, your father is male but you are, too," she says, a little sadly.

I nod. I've thought of it. But I have Schlegel genes, too. The men in Mom's family hang around forever. "I'm working on being the old-fashioned non-disposable kind," I say.

"Like cloth diapers?" She looks at me innocently.

I advance my hands like Frankenstein's monster's as if to clutch her neck. "Respect! You student of stagnant pond water. I speak in the name of science."

She cowers in fear but she spoils it a little by sticking her tongue out at me.

I do not think I am disposable as far as Riley is concerned. And that makes me feel very good.

I go off track several times and want to broaden the paper, but I can't. There's so much wonderful stuff like how nature plays tricks. Several orchid species resemble bees and wasps in the way they look, and they secrete chemical signals to evoke reproductive behavior in certain insects. The male insects try to mate with these orchids and that's how they pollinate them.

Then there's the male cricket. He produces a song attracting females by rubbing his "scraper" on one wing against his "file" on the other. Each cricket species has its own "song"; many can be singing at once but the right females hear and answer their own group's song.

I could go on and on. I read many wonderful things. Bean is also fascinated. We have to stop one another. We can't do it all. We make a million notes and then we come together for a mammoth weekend to organize this mishmash into a paper. We both have been compulsive in copying quotes, footnotes, and bibliographic references. Zygoda must not be able to say our paper is not honest scholarship.

We begin "Sexual Selection and Disposable Males: Two Aspects of Reproduction."

Sex is almost universal among living things; it is a fascinating subject to almost everyone, and its origins are still a mystery.

How or why did sex happen? Why didn't simple division (binary fission) continue in reproduction as in the amoeba? That way the offspring took all its genes from the parent. Division was easier. Sex took longer and took more energy. Was it an accident? We don't know, but it is possible that sex offered new genetic combinations. . . .

We wander on from the general to the particular and we struggle to keep it a manageable size.

What a weekend! We emerge still friends, but the friendship had some narrow squeezes.

We are too tired to do more than write an idiot conclusion. We hope Zygoda respects our work enough to forgive us for it.

The variety and pattern of courtship and mating in nature's creatures is fascinating and deserving of intense and prolonged study. After viewing just two small areas of nature's sexual complexity, *sexual selection* and *disposable males*, it is evident that binary fission is not even for the birds.

Sex is here to stay.

Some days start perfectly and then when you're relaxed and you've let your defenses down, wham, you get kicked in the butt.

This day starts with Mrs. Zygoda running into Bean and me in the entrance hall arid telling us our paper is an A; "a model" are her exact words. Would we object if she duplicated it before she returned it to us so there would be copies at the reference desk in the school library? "Your work is a valuable resource," she says.

I look at her and she is beautiful. The puckered mouth which I always thought looked much like that of a fish is at this holy moment positively sexy. All hail Mrs. Zygoda, Queen of biology.

Bean stares at me and I at him. "Yes, we object," we both say at once, and then we break up. "Of course we want you to put it in the library, Mrs. Zygoda," I say. "It would be an honor." Bean, as usual, overdoes it with a deep bow. Several kids passing by snicker. He couldn't care less. He bows again and snaps his running shoes together sharply. They don't click, they thud.

"I don't know how you clowns did such a superb job," the Queen of biology says, and takes off for the duplicating room.

Bean is immediately working on how we are a national resource and a natural resource as well as a valuable resource, and we are both light-headed with success. We knew it was a good paper but we needed that A to confirm it.

I float along on it all day. Lunchtime I share a meatball sandwich with Riley and I tell her about it. She's impressed but not overwhelmed. It seems stagnant water earned her an A as well. The topic wasn't spectacular enough to make the library collection, but Zygoda admired it two-pages-of-notes' worth.

"You ought to apply to some college for next year, Dave," Riley says. "You're too smart just to mark time."

"Seen my grades, Riley? Without SAT's or decent grades Dogcatcher U wouldn't let me major in rabies."

"I don't know. There are all kinds of schools. Some have flexible requirements, I bet."

"Not that flexible. Anyway, I was brought up to believe that when I go to college it has to be the best. Not to study a trade or anything technical, just to learn. To be challenged. That's Mom's word, as you might have guessed. She meant it. And I believe it. With my record now—if *I* were a good college *I* wouldn't take me."

Riley nods, but I know she doesn't really understand. She wasn't raised by a competitive father who always was a winner himself. It's bred in me as strongly as it's missing in her. She's planning on applying to Rutgers and to several other New Jersey state schools as backups. She'd love Rutgers to take her; she wants to stay near home and her folks and her gospel group.

Bean and I toss a basketball around during our free period. He's relaxed these days because St. John's has kissed him with a full scholarship.

College is all the time on his mind. He brings it up, too. Maybe it's a conspiracy between them or maybe each of them thinks of it independently, I can't tell. We're taking turns shooting baskets and I'm shooting wild but then, suddenly, I get the ball and run around and sink three—not one, not two, but *trois*—in a row. *Mon Dieu!* What a day!

"Not bad," Bean says.

Sheer envy.

"You're learning. Never give up. The best one may always be the next one." He pauses to breathe. "You ought to go see Zimmer today and get some senior info. Don't sit next year out."

Zimmer is Edison Regional's college adviser. Three computer-sent postal cards have come during the term telling me to come see him, but I have never darkened his door. There is no point in wasting the time of a college adviser if you don't want advice about college. And I didn't.

But today is different. Today I am one-half of a *valuable resource*. The part of me that I buried suddenly rises from the grave dug by divorce and wants to go to college. That part of me regrets that I was weak, that I screwed up and cut so much and missed the PSAT's and the early SAT's. Doing the paper with Bean was a blast. Biology is the greatest, most complicated puzzle around, and all the stuff I read was fascinating. My first time around with Henri Fabre, Charles Darwin, Stephen J. Gould, and E.O. Wilson. I could do that kind of reading and writing for the rest of my life.

As I'm showering and dressing in the locker room I decide I'll go give Zimmer a look. I don't have any great hope about him—his reputation stinks; even Riley who never bad-mouths anyone says you have to push Zimmer to make him go—

but he just might come up with a bright idea, an angle, a way we might get my oddball record considered. Zygoda would write me a reference. And maybe Aronson. Zimmer knows the schools and their rules. Is a broken home an extenuating circumstance? It should be, I think to myself as I neaten up for Zimmer. It's a handicap and all the schools are doing their best to be handicap-friendly. I need a broken-home ramp to glide in on.

Against my better judgment, I go.

"Who's that waiting over there?" Zimmer calls, peering over his glasses. He has his office door open inches.

Peekaboo. I see you, Zimmer. I watch him.

Zimmer is famous for never cracking the door open more than the width of his head if there's a student waiting outside. And he never emerges into the waiting area with its beat-up *Scholastic* magazines and piles of printed warnings about drug abuse. Though I have not been up here before I have heard the legends; he meets students only on his own turf. Rumor has it he's afraid of misadvised returnees. Who knows?

"Well, who are you?" Zimmer is irritated. I have no appointment.

"Dave Smith."

He looks doubtful.

"David Smith, Jr. Cloverdale."

"Why are you here, Smith?"

"You sent me cards."

The door shuts, him inside, me outside. It stays shut for a couple of minutes and then lo, Zimmer is there, holding a mysterious treasure in the tips of his fingers. It is my high school transcript, and he keeps it at a safe distance from his person in case it has a curse on it.

"Fourteen Forest Avenue?" he asks. "Ann and David Smith, parents?"

"Anna." I nod.

"I sent you three notices this semester—er—"

"Smith," I help him.

"Smith." He consults his watch. "Today is November twenty-fifth. To what do I owe this singular honor?"

To Bean, Riley, Henri Fabre, the praying mantis. To a lot of guys. I want to say it but I know enough to keep my big mouth shut. I shake my head to indicate that I have no answer. Like most little guys, Zimmer is big on the sarcasm.

He tips his head forward as if his neck suddenly gave. He does this so he can stare over his half-glasses. "Smith, an answer is expected."

"Sorry. I've been busy, Mr. Zimmer."

"Doctor." He points to the title on the door.

"I've been too busy, Doctor Zimmer." That's another thing I know about short guys. They need respect. They need to be dictators. In junior high school I had an English teacher who was about five feet tall and it killed him that I was bigger and I wrote good stuff. He used to take points off for every single little error, for a missing comma or a capital letter or even a fragment I wrote that way purposely for effect.

"Busy? Is that so?" Zimmer enjoys that. He gives me an all-tooth smile, the death grimace. Zimmer is one of those little men who eats too much and it all turns to fat. He's thin on the head fur but makes up for it in the eyebrows.

This is one ugly homunculus, I tell myself. It's hard to imagine that anyone could love Zimmer.

145

But there is a Mrs. Zimmer and three small Zimmers. Pictures of them stand on his desk and hang on the wall. Though trimmer, the kids are unmistakably Zimmers. I shudder at the thought of these junior Zimmers subject to this comedian who made it out of the classroom into college advisement.

Enough of that, I tell myself; if Zimmer can make it in this world, there is hope for all. I note with pleasure that he has the beginnings of wattles. I love that word. It was almost worth creeping through Dickens, eighth grade, two chapters a week with imbecilic questions at the end of each chapter, for *wattles* and *gaiters* and *choleric*.

"So you were busy. Too busy to plan your future, eh? That's pretty busy, I'll say." He waits for a response, but I can't even crack a smile. He's standing there catty-corner in the doorway playing piano on his belly, his vest of his three-piece brown corduroy suit riding up high. "What were you so busy doing, Mr. Smith? Meditating?" The tongue is curled; the pose is Johnny Carson.

Whatever I answer, Zimmer is going to pounce on.

"I don't know," I say. "Nothing," I mumble.

"Well, that's original. You go right ahead and do nothing for a bit longer, Smith. I'm busy now. You just wait."

The door closes.

Zimmer always makes everyone wait. He likes the power. Bean, Edison's king of the basketball court, once sat twenty minutes reading the drug warnings forward and then backward while he waited for Zimmer. When he got tired of sitting he took a high jump and looked through the transom, and he saw Zimmer sitting there clipping his fingernails. Bean just turned his chair upside down and strolled out of there and never went back. He doesn't have to worry, not with St. John's tucked into his pocket; that's his passport to the world.

The door opens. "Come," says the imperial voice. I go in. This big room is all crowded up with filing cabinets and benches and odd chairs and bookcases. Over the years whenever a piece of furniture became available, I think, Zimmer must have planted his flag. He's got inspirational messages on the wall aimed right at the heart.

> Training is everything. . . . cauliflower is nothing but cabbage with a college education.
>
> MARK TWAIN

I love it. It speaks to me in vegetable language.

Mens sana in corpore sano.

They must print these wholesale. They have the very same one in the gym. I asked Celantano about it and he really strutted because it's Italian—really Latin. He said the Romans believed that's what you need for true happiness: sound mind in a sound body.

Zimmer's signs gave me hope.

"Sit," he says. "You seem to have accumulated enough credits, Smith, to be a graduating senior. If you sit in your seat every school day till June and you don't kill anyone you will leave here." A fat smile shines on his face like grease. "We'll hope."

"I'll graduate," I say.

"Looking at this record I'd say it was time for you to enter the real world." Zimmer thumps the desk. "No use wasting your time and your family's

147

money with general schooling. Time to learn a trade, Smith. Or to enlist. Considered the army? The army instills discipline." He smiles.

"I'm against killing."

"No. And I thought you were a terrorist."

I don't care if he does make fun of me. How would he feel if a junior Zimmer's counselor who knew nothing about him counseled him into the military? On the basis of absences and failed courses. "My mother is a Quaker," I say. I want to be a cauliflower, I think.

I've shaken him up a bit. It's a stand-off. He waits. I wait.

"I'd like to go to a really good liberal arts college, Dr. Zimmer," I say quietly. It's honest, a feeler, gentle, humble.

It floors him. "You would? With that record?" He reads, "Thirty-seven absences and *those* grades? I notice you are a sometime athlete but you even managed to get a C in gym. How did you do that?"

"I didn't remember my white socks." Oh Zimmer, I pray, ask what happened to my grades, to me during my junior year. Look at the record and see the descent into Hell and ask me. See how I got destroyed. Ask me and I'll tell you. I'm not asking special favors. You have to understand.

He doesn't ask. Insanely, I decide to tell him anyway. As if that would make a difference. "My parents got separated and then divorced, Dr. Zimmer. That was part of my problem."

"I'm real sorry about that, Smith. It happens all the time these days. Almost every senior who comes to see me has a story like that. But you can't put that on your college application. There's no place for it. The computer doesn't want to know. We all have our troubles and we have to go right on trying to do our best."

I am sorry I told him. So sorry. The man doesn't *hear*.

"I'm curious," he says. "What made you think at this late date that you should dream the impossible dream?" His eyes are narrowed and he's got a little smile on his mouth.

"Biology" I say. "I've just discovered how much I like it."

"And you think any decent school is going to take note that David Smith in November of his senior year in high school discovered biology?" He is clearly outraged that I could dare think such a thing.

"I'd like to give it a try. I understand the odds aren't good."

He studies the record. "No tests. No SAT's. No achievements. And I suppose you haven't filed for the December SAT's?"

I shake my head.

"That's not the way it's done, Smith. We have a system. You know your Bible? Whatever a man soweth, Smith, that shall he also reap. For a long time you sowed nothing. How can you suddenly expect to reap?" He's looking at me as if I am a fungus on the tree of mankind.

"I was hoping you'd be able to think of some way I could try. There must be other people with special problems. Isn't there anything I can do?"

He picks up a pencil and taps the desk and waits a bit. "Look, Smith. You can go to a community college. Or a junior college. I can't think of a single first-rate institution that would consider you. But far be it from me to stop you. I do have to tell you, realistically, that you are not—according to this record—college material. Applications are expensive and time-consuming." He leans forward, hands on the corners of his desk, the sincere college adviser. "Let me talk to you the way I would to my own son. Do something practical. Train to be a travel agent; they're looking for smart people. Or take a course in computers."

"Biology," I say. "Science as a major in a good school. Maybe, eventually, in a couple of years, allowing me to transfer to Columbia."

"Pipe dreams. An exercise in futility. More busy work for Dr. Zimmer," he says, not pleasantly.

That's what they're paying you for, little man, I think, but I keep my yap shut. I feel totally abused. Zimmer has to process all the applications and transcripts and recommendations. I behave. I get up and I thank him for his time. "May I have SAT applications for the December exam?" I ask. "I hear they allow late registration."

He gives me the packet.

As I head for the door, he actually breaks down. "Good luck," he says. For one second I think a little better of him like he once might have been a human being. Then he can't resist. "You'll need it," he follows it up.

I crawl out of that interview grounded, on my knees. For a few stolen hours there, between Zygoda this morning and Zimmer, I did dream the impossible dream.

Riley insists that I file for the test. "What can you lose?" is her argument. "The scores stay on record. You can use them anywhere, anytime." She actually sits with me while I make out the forms and then she takes the stuff and mails it. So I've filed, but I've hit bottom.

I open the door with the fresh holly wreath on it and the warm house takes me in. We've got the tree standing in its usual corner near the fireplace. Tonight we'll take down the lights and wiring and check them out, and we'll unpack the ornaments. The angels and little old men and fat-faced dolls are old porcelain, very fragile. We need to be sure each is tight on its hook. A drop of epoxy expertly applied by toothpick does the job. I repaired a few last year. Mom tells me she's saving these ornaments for her grandchildren.

"Lady, you got a long wait. At least fifteen years," I tell her.

"Whenever. They're going to be remarkable when they come."

"Tall," I concede. "With very big feet." I already wear size thirteen. It's scary. As big as Frankenstein's monster.

Tomorrow I pick up my gift for her: a briefcase with her name engraved on it up near the handle: *Anna Schlegel Smith.* They're engraving the name in half-inch gold letters. The case is brown cowhide, large, so she can carry quantities of books and papers. The scent of the tree sweetens the front hall. I'm breathing it in as I pull off my boots, feeling at peace, when Mom comes in from the kitchen and lays it on me. "Your father phoned."

"So?"

"He's in New York."

The boot won't give. I pull at it violently. "Why?"

"He's come to see you."

"Well goody, goody." My face feels scalding hot. Now the boot flies off and hits the coat tree. It rocks. I look at her and—knowing he's in New York—I'm glad to see how nice she looks. Her fair, curly hair is cut short. Her red plaid pleated skirt and fuzzy gray sweater make her look like a student (which she is), and her face is relaxed and calm. She's looking real good—nothing like the rag doll the Big Man discarded a year ago.

"Who needs him to come back? We're doing all right now. He's going to upset everything."

"No, he's not. I can handle it, Dave." She sounds sure.

"I can, too. But I don't want to."

Long pause. "He's come a long way. I think you should see him."

"No one asked him to come."

"He came because he cares about you."

"Not enough." My voice is suddenly shrill. "He can just stuff it."

"Dave—"

"Now you're going to tell me to think about it. Quaker tactics. Okay. But I already know my answer. It's no."

I go upstairs and I'm really worked up. Why is he doing this? Someone who loves you and betrays you cancels out that love. A father who takes a powder should be sure it's a vanishing powder. He should disappear for good. Pffft! I don't want to see him or listen to him. I don't want to be with him. What do I care how far he's traveled? Lots of

152

strangers travel and he's a stranger to me now. He's outside my life.

Why didn't Mom slam the phone down? Out of character; she just wouldn't. But she could have said, "I don't want to talk to you. Dave doesn't want to see you. You are not welcome in this house. We are working on making other lives for ourselves and you have no place here. Not for an hour, not for a half hour, not even for a minute." He fouled unforgivably. He's out of our game. What a great sense of timing he has. Maybe this is an anniversary visit commemorating his departure. What else would bring him just now?

I get busy and develop some likely scenarios.

1

LAURIE: *(In a hospital bed, wasted, looking much older than Mom)* I know the truth. The doctor only gives me two weeks to live.

DAD: I asked him not to tell you.

LAURIE: I made him because I want to put things in order. This disease (hypergonadism, cancer, tuberculosis, leprosy, heart disease, brain tumor, elephantiasis) is my punishment for taking you away from your family, for stealing you.

DAD: Don't talk that way. If anyone should be punished it's me.

LAURIE: You suffer through me. You watch me and you know we did this wrong together. And you have suffered all along by being deprived of your wife—and your son. You don't know how he looks now,

153

how tall he is or how many push-ups he can do; how often he needs to shave or how good he's become on the basketball court.

DAD: He is a stranger to me now. What shall we do, Laurie?

LAURIE: Immediately after I die, I want to be cremated. I do not deserve a grave. I do not want to be remembered.

DAD: I will scatter your ashes from a plane over the frozen fields of this place where we made our false start.

LAURIE: Then go back home to them. Ask them to forgive you and me too. Try to be the Big Man you once were in their lives. *(Closes her eyes.)* Now I'm very tired. I want to rest.

2

LAURIE: *(Tight jeans, tight sweater, heavy make-up, high-heeled boots)* I've something to tell you, which may be a bit of a shock. I'm leaving you.

DAD: What? Why?

LAURIE: I'm bored. You're too old for me. I've found someone else.

DAD: A year ago you were madly in love with me. What's happened?

LAURIE: It's impossible to explain.

DAD: *(Agitated)* Try.

154

LAURIE: You know when someone falls in love . . .

DAD: Stuff it.

LAURIE: I know you don't understand it now. Some day you might. It's not that I don't care for you. But I care for him (Mike or Craig or Bruce or whatever) more. I love you like a father.

DAD: I don't see how you can do this.

LAURIE: I can't help myself.

DAD: Did you try?

LAURIE: *(Wry smile)* Not too hard.

DAD: I don't need you. I'll go back to my true family. They love me and will forgive me and take me back.

LAURIE: That's what you have wanted all along. I hear you in your sleep calling your son, all the time, always the same, "Dave. Dave, come see this fine clump of mushrooms." And then you wake, sweating. It's bizarre. He won't even write you a letter but he stays in your dreams. I'm sick of the whole thing.

DAD: You know what I'm sick of? The thought that I gave up two wonderful people, that I hurt them so badly for the likes of you. *(He exits. The door slams behind him, loudly.)*

3

LAURIE: *(Pale, in black dress, in a cemetery. Newly covered small grave; "Baby Smith" on*

155

marker) The doctor says the baby never had a chance.

DAD: I know. He was doomed from the start.

LAURIE: I wanted him to live. I didn't care about me but I wanted to give you a son to make up for the one I took you away from, the one you miss so much. *(Weeping)*

DAD: It's all right. We can try again. We can have other children.

LAURIE: No, we never will. I know that now. I see the loneliness in you, the need for your own flesh and blood, the need to be with your namesake and watch him grow.

DAD: Don't talk that way.

LAURIE: I must. Go back to them, David, to the people to whom you really belong. I borrowed you for a while but I was not meant to keep you.

DAD: Shh. You're just upset by this terrible thing. But it will pass.

LAURIE: I never meant anything more. I am living someone else's life. I can't go on doing it. I am not your true wife. It took the baby's death to show me that. *(Dad bends his head but does not deny her words.)*

I go back downstairs. "The answer is still no, Mom. I apologize for my rudeness before. But I won't see him. If you don't mind, I'll give dinner a pass tonight. Talking about him and then thinking about it made me sick. Sorry. Whenever you're ready we'll work on the tree stuff."

156

"Why don't you get started gluing?" she suggests.

"Good idea." It turns out to be a terrific idea. I wield the old toothpick and sticky stuff like Michelangelo. I'm good, real good. Quick and precise. Afterward, she joins me and we work side by side doing the lights and getting everything ready to hang. I have no idea what's going on in her head, but the inside of mine is one seething, boiling mass.

So—she tells him *no* when he calls back. She has to say it over four different times. She sticks with it firmly and her noes prevail. (I am tempted to grab the phone and tell him to leave us alone. But that would be talking to him, giving in to his whim.)

She hangs up. "He is as he was," she says, "unable to believe that it's no when he wants it to be yes. How can anyone say *no* to what he wants? This time he has to believe it. I think, finally, he accepts it. Tomorrow he'll be gone."

"That's an *extra* Christmas present for me," I say. "Good riddance."

Mom is silent, gathering up emptied boxes and bits of wire and string. "Remember charity," she says. "This is the season of charity—and love. Especially for losers, and this time *he* is the loser."

I look at her. She is hopeless. It's amazing how she survives at all in this crummy world. I kiss her on the cheek. "Merry Christmas, Mom, in advance. I predict it's going to be a great holiday."

Next afternoon I come home early so I can help with the tree. Mom hears my key and she's right on the other side of the door in her parka, hood up and zipped. "He's here," she says, her gray eyes bright with anger, "waiting in the living room. I've already said all I have to say to him. I'm going over to Marcia's. Call me when he's gone. I'll bring her back to supper and she can help us with the tree."

I follow what she's saying as if from inside the shower. There's interference. She goes out. She's been driven out, I think, of her own home. I pull off my boots. Which scenario will it be? I wonder. Which sad story will he ring in on me?

I am blazing hotter than any Yule log. I go in.

"Dave!" He is big, sitting on the couch, the monster amid the fragile ornaments and lights all piled carefully around him. He gets up and puts out his hand.

I'm a blind man. "Why'd you come?"

"To see you."

He's thinner and he looks good. I know the gray suit and the red tie. The blue button-down shirt is new. He's gone Yuppie. He never wore button-downs. There's no black crepe mourning band on his sleeve. The big gold bracelet sits on his wrist like a manacle. Plumage, I think. Courtship display. Bean would love it. I almost laugh. He is as he always was: oversized, muscular but lean, brown hair, brown eyes, decent nose. The Big Man. No signs of suffering or illness are detectable. He looks so much like me it's indecent.

"I didn't want to see you."

"So your mother told me rather emphatically. I came anyway."

"Okay. Now you've seen me."

Uncertainty flickers across his face for a second and then it's gone. The old self-confidence is back. "I want to talk to you," he says. "Don't be so sullen and pigheaded. I'm here after a year away and I have things to say to you."

"I'll be sullen and pigheaded and anything else I want. You forfeited the right to tell me how to behave."

"Sit down and listen," he says, "or I'll knock you down. I mean it." His hands are balled up and there are glints of anger shooting out of his eyes. Not that I'm afraid of him. I handled Mal Harris okay and if I hadn't been so cautious about my face so Mom wouldn't see bruises I could really have flattened him. It's just that I can't see us seriously going at one another. We are not that kind of family, not even now. And it would be sacrilege in Mom's living room.

"Good." He looks around for a seat. His old leather chair has been exiled so he settles for the edge of the couch again. He sits upright. "How are you?" he asks.

I almost laugh. "Terrific. I'm terrific."

"You've grown a lot. How tall are you?"

I shrug. "I don't know."

He takes a tape measure out of his pocket. I have trouble swallowing. He used to carry it there all the time and measure me at crazy times. Has he been carrying it all along? Did he remember to take it just before he set out this time? "Let's see," he says, and goes to the door frame nicked with pencil marks from all the other measuring ceremonies. Like a robot I follow his commands; I stand against the frame and he runs the tape out and makes the mark. "Six feet two and one-quarter," he says, and then he measures me again because he can't believe the growth since last time. Inside me, the line I practiced so long, *Hello, Tiny,* is bouncing around because at last I'm taller than he is and still going up. *Hello, Petite* is in there, but I shut it up tight.

"Pretty amazing," he says. "With height like that you must be one of the head honchos on the basketball team this year."

"I'm not on the team. Too many absences. Celantano wouldn't sit still for it."

A little nervous tic in his lower left cheek tells me how much that hurt him. The tic is new. I never saw it before.

"No basketball?" he says. "No basketball? I can't believe it. You lived for basketball." He shakes his head, uncomprehending.

"No more. I haven't played all year."

"How could you give up basketball?"

"It's nobody's fault," I say. "It just happened."

He recognizes the lines. Pocketing the tape, he sits back down on the couch. He's stunned.

"You didn't come all the way from Alaska and then force your way in here just to measure me. Why did you come?" I make myself comfortable in Mom's rocker.

You wouldn't think that's a hard question, but answering it takes him a while. "Actually, I did come for that, in a way. You're my son. You don't answer my letters. I wanted to see you, to talk to you, to see how you are, what you're doing."

I get up impatiently. He reads me. "I know. Now I've seen you and I've talked to you. But bear with me a little longer. Please sit down."

Reluctantly, I do as he asks.

"There are things I want to get straight with you, David. I know you don't forgive me yet."

"Never," I say. "Never."

The eyelids flicker. "Perhaps. I just want you to know that though it caused a lot of pain, I did the right thing. I love Laurie. I would have been living a lie if I didn't pull up and make my life with her."

I've got the rockets' red glare in my brain. This is one scenario that never occurred to me. He's happy! He's here to give me a progress report on his happiness. Who needs it? I hate it.

"I suppose you told Mom that, too. What do you want—applause?"

He flinches. "You've got a nasty tongue, son. No, I didn't tell your mother that."

"Don't call me 'son.' "

Now he's mad. His voice is lower and the words are slow and deliberate. "Don't be stupid. You are my son. Whatever happens, wherever you go. Even if your mother remarries that won't change. You are David Smith, Jr."

"I've got news for you. The name will be up for grabs. When I'm eighteen I am dropping the Smith, Jr. David Schlegel has more class. It's more distinctive. So you can have another kid and make him Junior."

He sits, hands between his knees, silent.

"As far as I'm concerned," I go on, "all it

161

means to be your son is to have bad genes. I can't change that so I'll have to fight them."

He studies me. "You're so incredibly bitter. Your mother has come to terms with the situation, but you? You're poisoned. She told me you were like this but I couldn't grasp it."

"Poisoned," I agree. "As if I'd eaten *Agaricus fastibilis.*"

"No. That would kill you instantly. Your bitterness and anger will slowly destroy your whole life if you let it."

"You got an antidote, Big Man?"

"Yes. Balance. Intelligence, which you have. Use it to try to understand. Forgiveness may be too much to expect from you, but understanding is necessary." He pauses and leans forward toward me. "A married man in his forties discovers that he is deeply in love. He hopes it will pass, that it is just middle-age hots. It doesn't pass. It gets worse. The young woman he loves loves him. They need one another to be happy. His life becomes a charade, all pretense, because there is a person he wants beside him and he is denying her. It's a dilemma. What should he do?"

"Look. You *did* it. This is *happily ever after* for you. What I don't get is why you are back here bugging me."

"Because I care about you. You're my son."

"Okay. Now you've seen me, you've seen how fine I'm doing. I'm doing terrific."

His body slumps as if he's tired. Maybe it's over. I hope so. But no, there's second wind; the Big Man does not give up easy. "What will you do after you graduate?"

"No plans."

"College? Columbia or one of the Ivy League

162

schools? Grandma left money for that. It's put away in trust for you."

"Riverside Memorial Chapel again, eh?" I deepen my voice. *"We make all final arrangements."*

He refuses to be baited. "Are you thinking of college?"

"I have a C average."

He stares. Phi Beta Kappa. Three major letters. The Big Man. "You had an A average a year ago."

"I got dumb."

"In a year?"

"It was a tough year. Some unexpected things happened. My father fell in love with long distances."

A lot of time passes with him huddling with his ideas trying to build a defense. "It's important," he manages at last, "to look ahead and try to make some tentative plans."

"Zimmer, the college adviser, thinks I should enlist in the army so they can make a man out of me."

He rubs his cheeks. "Not a bad idea. I learned a lot from my time in the military. It's a tough school but it sorts you out. Consider the marines. It's an elite corps."

Guess who had been a gung-ho marine? Never in battle but he had put in his time.

"My mother is a Quaker, remember? Some people care about principles. I'm not joining the military."

"There's no war on."

"There could be. The world is shaky: Central America, the Middle East, could blow."

"You're not talking principles," he says. "You're talking fear."

"There's that," I concede. "I don't want to die in Nicaragua or Lebanon."

Long silence. I decide to wind it up. "I'll find something to do with my life. Don't worry about me." I get up and he follows suit. My despair is too much for him.

I have a funny feeling of exhilaration suddenly. I'm glad he came! I'm glad he got a look at the extent of the damage. All that garbage about a man in his forties falls in love; what should he do? How should I know? That's not my question. I'm glad I got a look at how shallow he is. The Big Man. Life always hands over everything to him and it's never enough. Will I always care so much about him that knowing this hurts so?

"I'll be going." He heads for the hall. I follow him and stand by the stairs as he takes his London Fog off the peg and gets his long arms into it and buttons it up. Resolved: I will never own a trenchcoat. His hand on the doorknob, he turns. "Don't ruin your life to spite me," he says quietly, "because though it will hurt me it will destroy you. You're a smart and talented boy with a lot on the ball."

I keep my hands in my pockets. "I've got to work my own life out. When you pulled out of here it was for good as far as I am concerned."

"You'll make it," he says. "I have confidence in you. You're good stuff. And if ever—"

"Never. Never in a million years. What you did costs."

He looks at me and he's begging. "Don't change your name." It's almost a whisper. "Don't deny sixteen good years. And your grandmother. And me."

I'm floored. He cares that much. Okay, I'm a

164

sucker. Not of my own volition, I swear. Something inside me does it. I nod. "No sweat."

His eyes are wet. He goes.

I lock the deadbolt. Mom has her own key. I dial Miss McKuen's number to tell them that the coast is clear. "Open the windows, Dave," Mom says. "Air the place out. We'll be right home."

Upstairs, I start to wash up. Looking in the mirror I see a tired young copy of his face. Nothing to be done about it short of plastic surgery. This is the way I look.

Wherever did I get the dumb idea that there is justice in the world? He isn't suffering terribly. He's pretty happy. My father is the original have-your-cake-and-eat-it kid. The only thing he didn't get was all the icing. Me. So he'll have to learn to do without me. 'Cause he's got all he is ever going to get.

I'm not sorry I caved in over the name. They *were* sixteen good years and I did love Grandma Smith very much.

Will he ever learn? Or when he's a very old man will he still be spooking me with those letters in pale blue airmail envelopes that I send back unopened?

While I'm rinsing my face in cold water, I make up my mind to put it all down on paper like so many of those other guys whose fathers eluded/deserted/mistreated or simply died on them: Dickens, Poe, Keats, Melville, Hawthorne, London, Byron, Stevenson, Kafka. And Tennessee Williams.

Not that I'm a great writer or anything like that. I just have to get it down fast and honest.

It's the half day, December twenty-fourth, and the school building is jumping with pre-holiday noise.

Riley and her gospel group are strolling the corridors singing carols. To my amazement, Adriana is singing with them. The pink is gone from her hair and though she is wearing three earrings in one ear and one earring in the other ear she looks pretty normal. Their music is *terrific*. All the kids stop to listen, and they applaud madly. Teachers, too.

I go see Dean Packard and he's swamped with Christmas packages and his phone is ringing like a burglar alarm. But he makes a little time for me. Briefly I tell him of my predicament and my idea to put it all down. He considers it and he warms to it. "Yes," he says, "good idea. Use the winter break to put it all on paper and then we'll see what we can do. Understand, I can't promise you anything?"

"I understand."

"I don't suppose you've sent for any college applications, Smith?"

I shake my head.

"Wait here," he says. "I have an idea." He zips out of there. Ten minutes later he's back with three college catalogues and their application packets. "Dr. Zimmer's samples," he chuckles. "He didn't want to part with them but I asked him where his Christmas spirit was." He sorts the material. "See— one Ivy application. One small first-rate school. One second-rate safety school—with a pretty good biology program." He unfolds an application form and looks it over. When he gets to page four, he's excited. "Look," he says, delighted, "they're asking for it. Go for it."

His handshake is more wrestler than dean. I respect that kind of handshake.

I like his style.

I decide to do it, to gamble on an admissions

officer—with compassion—reading what I write. And if there is no such species, or if natural selection has eliminated all such admissions officers and kept on only heartless computer types? I have to take my chance.

I won't enlist because that's what Zimmer advises and Zimmer couldn't care less about me.

NO SATISFACTION FOR ZIMMER!

I won't enlist because my mother's son has no place in the military.

I won't give up hope. I'll hang in there until whatever is happening gets better.

I won't hide anywhere. I won't duck. And I'm not running.

Drying my face, I resolve that David Smith, Jr., will try to become a new man.

Maybe not a new man. But, with any luck, a freshman.

ABOUT THE AUTHOR

SHEILA SOLOMON KLASS, who lives in Leonia, New Jersey, is the author of *Nobody Knows Me in Miami, To See My Mother Dance, Alive and Starting Over,* and *The Bennington Stitch,* as well as several novels and novellas for adults and a memoir about life in Trinidad. Mrs. Klass is a professor of English at the Borough of Manhattan Community College in New York City.

Special Offer
Buy a Bantam Book
for only 50¢.

Now you can order the exciting books you've been wanting to read straight from Bantam's latest catalog of hundreds of titles. *And* this special offer gives you the opportunity to purchase a Bantam book for only 50¢. Here's how:

By ordering any five books at the regular price per order, you can also choose any other single book listed (up to a $5.95 value) for only 50¢. Some restrictions do apply, so for further details send for Bantam's catalog of titles today.

Just send us your name and address and we'll send you Bantam Book's SHOP AT HOME CATALOG!